Bread of Life Discourse

A Meditation on Chapter Six of St. John's Gospel

Arthur X. Deegan II, PhD

BREAD OF LIFE DISCOURSE

Copyright © 2015 Arthur X. Deegan II, PhD.

All rights reserved. No part of this book may be used or reproduced by any means, graphic, electronic, or mechanical, including photocopying, recording, taping or by any information storage retrieval system without the written permission of the publisher except in the case of brief quotations embodied in critical articles and reviews.

iUniverse books may be ordered through booksellers or by contacting:

iUniverse
1663 Liberty Drive
Bloomington, IN 47403
www.iuniverse.com
1-800-Authors (1-800-288-4677)

Because of the dynamic nature of the Internet, any web addresses or links contained in this book may have changed since publication and may no longer be valid. The views expressed in this work are solely those of the author and do not necessarily reflect the views of the publisher, and the publisher hereby disclaims any responsibility for them.

Any people depicted in stock imagery provided by Thinkstock are models, and such images are being used for illustrative purposes only. Certain stock imagery © Thinkstock.

ISBN: 978-1-4917-6014-7 (sc)
ISBN: 978-1-4917-6013-0 (e)

Printed in the United States of America.

iUniverse rev. date: 02/04/2015

Dedication

This short Scripture study
is prayerfully dedicated
to my lovely wife, Patricia
whose dedication to Jesus
in the Eucharist
has been an inspiration to me
for over 50 years

Acknowledgement

Scripture texts in this work are taken from the New American Bible, revised edition, @ 2010, 1991, 1986, 1970 Confraternity of Christian Doctrine, Washington, D.C. and are used by permission of the copyright owner. All rights reserved. No part of the New American Bible may be reproduced in any form without permission in writing from the copyright owner.

Foreword

Chapter Six of the Gospel of St. John is one of the most important chapters in the books of the New Testament. It has long been considered the treasury of the Eucharist. It consists of two parts: first, the story of the multiplication of the loaves and fishes, and second, Our Lord's discourse on the Bread of Life, recognized by His followers as referring to the Eucharist.

The miracles and sayings of Jesus were handed down by word of mouth in the Christian communities; they were meditated upon long before the gospels were written down.

As the multiplication story was passed down, the Christian people were increasingly struck by the connection between this miracle and the central Christian mystery, the Eucharist. They began to see a close parallel in gesture and wording between the multiplication and the Last Supper.

Think of what the priest says and does in consecrating

bread and wine at Mass. Now watch Jesus in multiplying the bread and fishes: He took the loaves and looking up to heaven, He gave thanks, blessed them and gave them to the disciples to set before the crowd; and they all ate and were satisfied.

Now that multiplication was not the Eucharist. But the gospels see this miracle as a sign. It fulfilled the Old Testament promise that in the days to come God would feed His people with plenty. And it looked forward to the Last Supper and all subsequent suppers when Christ would feed his sisters and brothers with the food that gives everlasting life.

In the second part of Chapter Six, our Lord's discourse on the Bread of life has been one of the most difficult to grasp. The author of this book, Dr. Arthur Deegan, does not claim to set forth hitherto unknown meaning of the words of St. John. Rather, his intent is to suggest that meditating on these oft-read words may reveal an aspect of what Jesus is teaching as a new thought, a new idea to bring the reader closer to Jesus.

The author presumes to set forth what he thinks might have been going on in the mind of one follower of the Master. He selects as this disciple St. Joseph of Arimathea, a learned Jewish leader, open-minded and objectively trying to assess the validity of Jesus' claim to be the Way, the Truth and the Life, who would therefore ponder in his heart what he sees and hears.

I strongly recommend this novel treatment of the study of scripture. Individuals will find it helpful in their devotion to the Eucharist and bible study groups will find it a tool for useful discussion.

Rev. Msgr. Michael F. Devine
Pastor Emeritus, St Brendan Parish
Clearwater, Florida

Introduction

✝ Chapter Six of the Gospel according to St. John has long been considered the treasury of the Eucharist, in that it contains Our Lord's discourse on the Bread of Life, recognized by his closest friends at the time (and by millions of His followers down through the centuries) as being the words of eternal life. This chapter has also been one of the most difficult to understand, giving way finally to an assent of Faith on our part, as indeed was required from his listeners many of whom simply gave up, complaining "This is a hard saying".

There have been countless books, homilies, papal encyclicals, and erudite works of all kinds seeking to make the lessons of this chapter of St. John more inspirational, if not more intelligible to us. The purpose of this writing is not to set forth a hitherto unknown meaning of the words of St. John. Rather, knowing that multiple readings and meditations on these holy words can always find ways to mine new insights into the message of the evangelist, my intent is to offer a way for this to happen.

Scripture scholars – sometimes called exegetes – have suggested that we might best profit from our study of the gospels by taking it in two distinct steps. First, since St. John and the other evangelists were writing a history, we should attempt to understand the events being recorded as actual occurrences. This might be done by trying to see and hear them through the eyes and ears of people witnessing them at that time. Second, since the writers, as instruments of the Holy Spirit, were also giving us inspired words, we should then inquire for ourselves "What do these events mean to me and my life?"

I am therefore offering a meditation on Chapter Six of St. John in two parts. In Part One I ask you to watch what Jesus does and hear what he says as might have been done by one of his followers.

Unfortunately, unlike modern communication technologies, which give us "live" coverage of events and discourses, there is no record or testimony left to us by such a bystander. On the other hand, the cynic among us might say "Thank God we do not have the countless analysts of those very same modern media which befuddle us with contradictory 'reports' so that we are not sure they are describing the same events!" Better that we are left to our own efforts to imagine what someone listening to Jesus might have thought about what Jesus said and did in St. John, chapter 6.

I therefore presume to set forth here what I think

might have been going on in the mind of one such follower of the Master. I take this disciple to be a learned Jewish leader, open-minded and objectively trying to assess the validity of Jesus' claim to be the Way, the Truth and the Life. As such he would ponder in his heart what he sees and hears. The word "ponder" is taken here to mean not only reflecting in one's mind, but as the derivation of the word suggests, a give and take, an argument with oneself to determine the full meaning of what is pondered. As the subject for this mind reading, I have chosen a man mentioned in the gospels as a follower of Jesus, Joseph of Arimathea, who might very well have been present for these happenings, though we have no record that he was actually there. The absence of such a record only emphasizes the imagining of everything that follows, for whatever it might be worth.

What you will read in Part One is part history and part fiction. The italicized words are true history, the life of Jesus as recounted and translated in The New American Bible. The rest is pure fiction of my imagination.

In Part Two of this volume, you will find the "pondering" of a present day follower of Jesus, reflecting on what we now know this chapter of St John was referring to, namely the Blessed Sacrament. A conversation with Jesus about His words in Chapter Six is a way of answering the question "What do these events mean to me and my life?"

Reading the mind of Joseph of Arimathea in Part One and conversing with Jesus as a modern-day follower of Him in Part Two can offer new insights into this difficult chapter of St. John's gospel. But my years of teaching at the university level bore more fruit when helping students reach their own conclusions about our subject matter if they were given challenging questions to answer on their own. I therefore have provided the reader, or bible study group, two or three pointed questions after each section of my text. Adhering to the rule that there are no right or wrong answers to such questions can stimulate deeper insights for the individual or thoughtful discussions among members of a group.

The questions also provide an opportunity to pause and reflect on just a sentence or two of the gospel account at a time. This way what was said or done can sink in and give some credence to the assumption posited here that Joseph was really wrestling with the question of who this Jesus was. That in turn may help the reader to follow the step-by-step probative sequence in accepting Jesus as the Son of God.

By these means we hope to find ever-new insights into the words of the gospel. This does not mean finding a personal, private interpretation of what the evangelist is saying. We want our investigation to be guided by what tradition and the teaching of the Church have taught us about these events.

A Disciple of Jesus

Joseph of Arimathea is venerated as a saint by the Roman Catholic, Eastern Orthodox, Lutheran and some Anglican churches. His feast day is March 1 in the traditional Catholic liturgical calendar, but is now listed, along with Saint Nicodemus, on August 31 in the Roman Martyrology.

He is principally remembered as the one, according to all four canonical gospels, as the man who donated his own prepared tomb for the burial of Jesus after His crucifixion. He and Nicodemus came out of hiding and clearly aligned themselves with Jesus at His death, even though they might have thought His movement had come to an end. They had nothing to gain and everything to lose, being important members of the Jewish leaders. Their request for the body of Jesus was a very courageous act.

Joseph had no claims on the body and put himself in considerable danger, depending on how Pilate viewed his request. We know that Pilate had clearly said three times that he found no guilt in Jesus, and seemed to be trying to get the Jewish mob to ask for the release of Jesus. This may account for his allowing Joseph to take the body.

But who was this interesting man? What do we know about him? In Mark 15:43 we read that Joseph was a "distinguished member of the council (Sanhedrin), and was himself awaiting the kingdom of God". In Matthew 21:57 we read he was a "rich man, a disciple of Jesus". In Luke 23:50-51 we read that Joseph "though he was a member of the council, had not consented to their plan of action" (the death of Jesus).

Joseph's being a rich man accounts for him having a "rock-hewn tomb in which no one had yet been buried" (Lk 23:53). Some have interpreted Joseph's role as fulfilling

Isaiah's 53:9 prediction that the grave of the "Suffering Servant" (the Messiah) would be that of a rich man.

Among early Christians a mass of legendary, but unsubstantiated, detail was accumulated around the figure of Joseph in various apocryphal and non-canonical accounts. For example, Saint John Chrysostom (347-407), the Patriarch of Constantinople, in his "Homilies on the Gospel of St. John", thought that Joseph was one of the seventy two disciples appointed by Jesus in Luke's tenth chapter to go two by two to preach the word.

More fanciful accounts in the middle ages spoke of a goblet of Blood collected by Joseph from the crucified Jesus as the holy grail that inspired the Arthurian legends.

But let us return to the gospel-based Joseph of Arimathea. How did he come from awaiting the kingdom of God – as were many good believers in the Old Testament – to being strong enough to be the nay-sayer among the members of the Sanhedrin plotting the death of Jesus? How did he become a disciple of Jesus and find that kingdom in the person of Jesus?

Pope Benedict XVI spoke often about a Christian as one who has come to a definite direction in the course of his life because of an encounter with the Christ. Perhaps that is what happened to Joseph. Being a disciple of the Master, but secretly for fear of the Jews (Jn 19:38), we can assume he was a follower of the itinerant Preacher during His public ministry, always waiting and looking for, the kingdom of God. His openness to the message of Jesus eventually became an encounter that shaped the rest of his life.

What follows in Part One is an imagination of what might have been going on in the mind of this secret disciple/ follower of Jesus during this series of important events in the public life of Our Lord. I invite you now to put on your ESP faculties and listen to the pondering (arguing with self) of Joseph of Arimathea as he accompanied Jesus.

PART ONE – THE MUSINGS OF JOSEPH

The Multiplication of the Loaves and Fishes

> *After this, Jesus went across the Sea of Galilee (of Tiberias). A large crowd followed him, because they saw the signs he was performing on the sick. (Jn 6:1-2)*

Oh Teacher, have pity on these old bones of mine. Young as you are, you do not find it difficult to cross the Sea. Of course, the Twelve carry you every where in their boats, so you may not appreciate how the rest of us have to struggle to keep up with you. But I remember what you said just after you cured the royal official's son: "Unless you people see wonders, you will not believe" (Jn 4:48). That had certainly been a wonder! You cured that boy even though you were nowhere near him at the time. I never heard of such a thing. No doctor or wonder-worker has ever produced a cure "long distance" as you did, telling the father to go home because his son was all right. Even time and distance seem to be subject to your command.

Yes, we continue to follow you because you perform such works, especially because you claim they are not your own doing, but that of your Father. I must hear more of this.

And no one has ever challenged the law of the Sabbath as you did shortly thereafter at the Sheep Gate, the pool at Bethesda when you told the crippled man "Rise, take up your mat and walk" (Jn 5:8). You apparently wanted us to know you are the Lord of the Sabbath as you are Lord of time and distance. No wonder my colleagues in the Sanhedrin tried all the more to kill you for breaking the Sabbath and calling Jahweh your Father. Are you here telling us plainly that you are equal to God?

Yes, after seeing the signs that you work, I must continue to follow you. You insist you cannot do anything on your own. You are committed to seeking only the will of the one who sent you. Who is that, Teacher? I have seen you talking to no one like that! You rebuked us for not believing unless we see signs and wonders. But is that not the way Jahweh has always convinced our forefathers to accept his prophets?

We are only human, Rabbi. How often I have acknowledged that and explained signs in our rabbinical classes. We need all kinds of signs. There are signs that tell us our location; there are signs that warn us of nearby dangers; there are signs that point us in a direction; there are signs that state the rules we must follow. But most important, there are signs that are a proof of what is being claimed, that indicate the truth of something, that are the outward manifestation or symptom of something invisible, or that are a foreshadowing of something great to follow. We have been taught, Teacher, to watch for such signs so that we not be misled, so that we will recognize the kingdom when it is to come. I long for that kingdom. So I joyfully follow you as you teach us by these signs as you now fully acknowledge our weakness. Surely you will continue to show us by signs that it is you who are the prophet Moses told us would come. And so many of us continue to follow you now across the sea.

<u>Questions</u>

Why did Jesus rebuke the Jews for not believing in Him unless they saw signs and wonders?

Did not the prophets and the kings of the Old Testament use signs and wonders to convince the Israelites that they were messengers of God?

> *Jesus went up on the mountain, and there he sat down with his disciples. The Jewish feast of Passover was near. (Jn 6:3-4)*

Merciful Father in heaven, how good it is to sit down and rest awhile. Crossing the sea, scaling even this small rise in the landscape – Teacher, I do not know how much longer I can keep up with you. Maybe you plan to take it easy now with the Passover being near. We have been wondering if perhaps you intend to take just a few of us on a brief holiday from your hectic pace of preaching and curing the sick. We have earned a brief respite so we can celebrate the feast in peace and quiet.

But, oh, oh, look at the mob who went around the shore and has now caught up with us. That can only mean more teaching on your part, for you never miss an opportunity to talk to us about your Father. You have no thought about rest for yourself, arduous as it is to keep up this avalanche of words about love and compassion. No, you only think of how hungry we are for your words.

Questions

Can you imagine how tired Jesus must have been after the hectic pace he kept while preaching the Kingdom of God and curing the sick?

Why do you think the crowd followed Jesus around the shore?

> *When Jesus raised his eyes and saw that a large crowd was coming on him, he said to Philip "Where can we buy enough food for them to eat?" He said this to test him, because he himself knew what he was going to do. (Jn 6:5-6)*

Forgive me, Teacher, for thinking of them as a mob. They are indeed large in number and not orderly in their desire to catch up with you. They are not as fortunate as I am to be numbered among your daily followers. But see how you love them all. Tired as you are of such a crowd pressing upon you; careful as you were to escape across the sea and assure a haven on this hill top; you immediately think of their needs, knowing they (and we) have been following you for some time and must be hungry. You are always thinking of others. Apart from your signs and wonders, certainly your thoughtfulness and love of others is a sign you are close to God, if not sent by him.

And now you speak to the Twelve about buying food for this great mob – er, crowd. So your first concern for them is not what else you can teach them, but rather what you can do to meet their immediate bodily needs. My goodness, I know you have a little money, kept by Judas, to pay for small things and to give to the poor. But to buy food for so many! Good thing you addressed Philip and not Judas. The latter would have spit nails at such a thought, so miserly is he in keeping your treasury. We in the Sanhedrin would never attempt to feed so many. We would send them home!

I don't know why you are testing Philip with this question. Is he supposed to read your mind and know what you want to do, because he has been one of your followers for so long? I am sure I would not know how to answer your question, should you give me that same test. Come to think of it, you have never yet given me a test, or even spoken directly to me about anything. I sense you respect my desire to follow you, yet "in the shadows", so to speak.

I can see the twinkle in your eye as you ask Philip about this. You must have some idea of what should be done. Are you going to prove you are the Son of God, a prophet greater than Moses, by calling down manna from heaven as was done for our fore-fathers? That would be a sign all right to prove to even the worst scoffer that you have been sent by God. You told us before that we ask for a sign, but no sign will be given to us. We have the words of Moses and the prophets, and if they are not good enough, then you can't help that! Still, even I would be a lot more comfortable, Rabbi, if you would do something wonderful in our sight, so that we could all believe in you.

Questions

What do you think was meant by Jesus' putting Philip "to a test"?

Is there any logic on the part of Joseph to begin to think of God feeding the Israelites with manna from heaven?

> *Philip answered him "Two hundred days' wages worth of food would not be enough for each of them to have a little!" (Jn 6:7)*

Just what I thought, Philip. A day's wage is now about one denarius. Two, or maybe even three hundred denarii would not feed this crowd (including all of us). But, Philip, you ought to know not to present the Lord with such an answer. He did not ask you how much it would cost. He asked where you could spend whatever it might cost. And, of course, out here where we are, away from any town, Jesus certainly knew the answer to his own question. I can see the flabbergasted look on your face, Philip, because you quickly turn to Andrew.

You know your answer is not one to be of very much help. Your immediate instinct then is to get help from others of the Twelve. And Andrew, being among the first followers of our Teacher, is probably in a position to know what Jesus is looking for by way of an answer.

Questions

Why do you think Philip turned to Andrew in trying to answer the question Jesus put to him?

Who were the first two followers of Jesus and how did they come to be such?

> *One of his disciples, Andrew, the brother of Simon Peter, said to him "There is a boy here who has five barley loaves and two fishes; but what good are those for so many!" (Jn 6:8-9)*

Yes, Andrew comes to your rescue, Philip. So Jesus turns his attention away from you, since you failed his test! You should have known that the Teacher had his own way of dealing with this situation, that he will doubtless use it to further his instructions to us. And even you, Andrew, are close to being impertinent, asking the question of Jesus, "What good are they for so many?" Or maybe it was a rhetorical question. Maybe you are smart enough to know that Jesus had that all figured out for himself. I wonder if I will ever be so convinced of the divinity of Jesus that I could be as trusting as you, Andrew, and the rest of the Twelve, to never doubt he is always in charge, always knowing what he will do. How long must I continue following him, in so many different situations, seeing him teach by the works of the one he calls his Father? Now I see Jesus motioning to the two of you and the rest of us who are closest to him.

I wonder how Andrew came to know about this boy. Was that the child's own lunch that he and perhaps his father and brothers were about to eat, having had the foresight to know they would be far from home or other eating location? Were there others with similar provisions? Maybe the Teacher is going to ask for volunteers to share their personal food with others, sharing being an important element of his teaching? Are we to help encourage such sharing in this large crowd?

Questions

Do you think the boy with the loaves and fish volunteered to give them over to Andrew (and Jesus)?

Could there have been other similar provisions among so large a crowd?

> *Jesus said "Have the people recline". Now there was a great deal of grass in that place. So the men reclined, about five thousand in number. (Jn 6:10)*

OK, Master, you want us to get a little organization in this crowd. If you are going to do something about their number, starting with those few loaves of bread and fish, we better make sure there is some semblance of order in the way they recline. Maybe in groups small enough to move about within them, and not so many groups that they are too far from you? How about 100 groups of 50? That will take care of the 5000 men. There seem to be a few women and children also, but mostly among those who have been among our number for quite some time. Seems the majority of this crowd are new to me, rather recent curious followers.

Jesus, as you look upon the great crowd you see the heat of the day begin to overtake us. The gentle breeze that rose with the noon hour carries the smell of fresh grass to your sensitive nostrils. As a youth you worked in your foster-father's carpentry shop, but had you ever taken sheep to pasture and learned to associate grass with their eating? And now, as a shepherd, does breathing the rich fragrance of the grass cause you to realize that the crowd has not eaten all day, for listening to your words? Some of the Apostles want to dismiss the people that they might buy bread in the nearby towns and villages, but that is too harsh for you, so you say "Have the people recline."

O gentle Jesus, Your kindness moves you to have pity on these people who listened to you. After feeding our minds, you would not send us away without physical nourishment. Your bounty is boundless. If you have to, will you perform a miracle to show your compassion? Will you? In your own body you had felt the hunger of the poor, our thirst, our exhaustion. You had a part in our sweat, our tears, our exhaustion. And so you make us recline. There must be nothing taxing, nothing strenuous in partaking of whatever banquet you have in mind.

Anyway, we now have the crowd down on the grass. I feel I made a contribution myself. They mostly do not know who I am, but I have been able to show a little leadership in helping the Twelve get the people down in reasonable order and comfort.

Questions

Do you think it would have been only natural for Joseph to try to help the Twelve in getting some order in this crowd?

Can you see him going from a secret follower to an active assistant in ministering to the crowd?

> *Then Jesus took the loaves, gave thanks, and distributed them to those who were reclining, and also as much of the fish as they wanted. (Jn 6:11)*

Well, I guess I was wrong again in my trying to guess what you would do. You do not ask for others to surrender their meager food, should they have any. Instead you are doing something with the child's loaves and fish. You raise your eyes to heaven and bless the few pieces of bread. You want the Twelve to pass them out as afar as they will go. I don't know how many people so few loaves will feed, but we begin to do as you instruct.

Again I am grateful for being able to help you in this distribution, Master. But it is hard to pay attention as we pass the food out because, miracle of miracles, the loaves

Bread of Life Discourse

and fish seem to be without number. No sooner do we give some to part of the crowd than there is more of the same for the next few persons. How can this be? And there is no grabbing, no confusion, no fighting to be sure their hunger is satisfied. Everyone seems to be happy with what was passed to them.

I myself reclined after I helped distribute this largesse, and I'm not sure where the food I ate came from: it just was there for me to eat. Not that this creaking old bag of bones of mine needs a lot to eat, but there it was, all I wanted, and plenty left over all around me. This has truly been a multiplication of those initial loaves and fish. Must have come from the hands of Jesus after he blessed it. He always begins a meal giving thanks to his Father, as he did here. He did not particularly ask his Father for anything, as far as I could see. Yet somehow there was no end to what he had to distribute.

Well, I wondered what Jesus would do. And he did not disappoint me. I had heard about the first wonder that he did, back in Cana of Galilee, when he was at a wedding feast. I was not there myself, but hearing what I did is what spurred me to begin to follow the Master. As the story goes, he was there with his mother, Mary, when the groom ran out of wine long before the week-long festivities were to end. And they would have ended disastrously if something had not been done about the insufficient amount of wine they had on hand. But the day was saved when the wine steward found a fresh supply of new wine of a much better quality than they had at first.

Rumor has it that it was Jesus who somehow told the servants where to find this new wine. Some even say Jesus had instructed the servants to fill ordinary water jars with water and from those same jars came the new wine! That in turn caused some to say he had changed the water into wine, impossible as that might be. I did not know what to make of that story, which is one reason I decided to start following you, Master. I have witnessed some of the cures you have worked on the poor and destitute, but I have been waiting for something akin to the Cana story to show you had power over material things. With the loaves and fish, you have now done it! While I cannot explain how it happened, I must confess you made it happen. I did not just imagine it. I ate along with the thousands here. You are truly blessed by Jahweh.

While I have seen this take place right in front of me and it helps me put more trust in you and how you exhort us to live, I wonder if the significance of what has taken place is grasped my many in the crowd. Surely those up front near us saw that there was no large cache of bread and fish being broken into and distributed. But most of the groups of 50 are too far away and simply accepted what was handed to them without bothering to ask where it all came from. And that does not seem to bother you. You fed the crowd and did not ask to be thanked. You worked a miracle and did not make any bones about it. You showed your loving care for this hungry "mob" but did not make a spectacle of it. How different you are from those who tithe and brag about it, who show mercy to the poor but make them never forget who their donors are! Yes, it is such a humble, generous benefactor as you whom I wish to follow.

Questions

Why would it be only natural if Joseph were reminded of the rumored miracle at Cana in connection with this miraculous feeding of five thousand?

What impact do you think this miracle had on Joseph and his search for the Messiah?

> *When they had had their fill, he said to his disciples "Gather the fragments left over, so that nothing will be wasted". So they collected them, and filled twelve wicker baskets with fragments from the five barley loaves that had been more than they could eat. (Jn 6:12-13)*

I guess I'm not the only one with extra food around me. For the Master instructs us to gather up all that is left in the entire crowd. He does not want to waste any. How thoughtful again. He knows there are others who are hungry along the way we shall pass. So every scrap of "left-overs" was collected so that a dozen baskets are needed to hold them all.

I had thought earlier that Jesus might call down

manna from heaven. I don't know if that is where this feast came from. But I see that we are to care for it as assiduously as did our fore-fathers when the manna of Moses greeted their eyes of a morning. I can't help but think of both of these heavenly breads in the same breath. I wonder if there is more of a connection than that.

I have been trying to put aside the bias against Jesus that all of us in the Sanhedrin have had. I have been trying to keep an open mind to find justification for the things he has said and done that infuriated all the elders. I have been trying to see if he really is breaking the law of Moses and thereby deserving of the hatred now burning in the minds of his enemies. But when I see things like this feeding of five thousand, I am at my wits end to explain it. It certainly does make him look like a sorcerer to the casual observer. On the other hand, I can see how enamored of him are all these people who have just feasted. Will they now go home at the end of this day's journey?

Questions

As Joseph continued to "argue with himself" while pondering the miracle he has just witnessed, which side of the argument seems to be winning at this point?

What might make some in the crowd see this as the work of a sorcerer?

> *When the people saw the sign he had done, they said "This is truly the Prophet, the one who is to come into the world." (Jn 6: 14)*

Oh, I see. Many of the people have recognized, as I did, that this has been a wonder performed in front of their eyes. They see it as a sign, or proof, of Jesus' claim to have been sent by the Father as the great Prophet promised by Moses. Jesus did not say that here, though at many other times he described himself as being "sent". I guess their superstitious minds do not need any logical reasoning, but just jump to the conclusion that is easiest to arrive at, and that will lead them to do something spectacular in return, something radical, something of a purely emotional nature. Yes, I see them already, jumping up from their positions on the grass, milling around Jesus with shouts of Hosanna.

Some of them are even openly calling you the Prophet promised by Moses. I'm not sure I can follow their logic here. Was the Prophet supposed to feed their bodies? Was the Prophet going to identify himself by a miracle of nature like this? They did not seem to recognize the wisdom and holiness of your teaching, even when you saw them down on the side of the mountain and explained how blessed are the meek, the pure of heart, the care takers of their brethren. So their Hosannas here seem to be based only on feeding their bellies.

Why does the rabble always act spontaneously? How easy it is for a few loud mouths to stir up passions, for good or bad, of an ignorant mob! Oh, there I go again, Master, demeaning the ones you love. But I see you are not welcoming their adulation, are you?

Questions

How realistic is Joseph's assessment of the crowd at this point?

Would you have reacted in the same way as those in the crowd?

> *Since Jesus knew that they were going to carry him off to make him king, he withdrew again to the mountain alone. (Jn 6:15)*

See, I was right. You have disappeared from our midst. A moment ago you were seeing to it that the extra food was being harvested for some good purpose. But sensing that this raucous crowd was about to do something impetuous, you are gone. Good thing – you probably would have been crushed in the midst of those foolhardy revelers. I hope no one gets hurt! They seemed intent on interfering with your plans by forcing their devotion upon you. What did you say on similar occasions, something like "My time has not yet come"? I'm not sure what that means, but it is clear now that you have your own ideas as to what shall happen next, so you have moved on alone. Even the Twelve are looking around helplessly trying to see where you have gone.

It is beginning to dawn on me that you have not

come to be any kind of temporal ruler. On more than one occasion similar to this, the crowd would have gladly, through you, restored the kingship of Israel. But you melt into the hillside and avoid their well-meaning Hosannas. If you have been sent by the Father, then it seems our hope should no longer be for a Messiah to free us from the bondage of the Roman occupation force. Your mission is quite something else, more like the prophets of our forefathers who were not exalted because of battlefield deeds, but because of their teachings full of love and compassion. You certainly have exhibited a lot of those traits. At any rate, we don't know where you whisked yourself off to, but, having been refreshed by the munificence of your banquet on he hillside, I am ready to listen to more of your teachings.

Questions

What do you think Joseph thought at this point with regard to his longing to find the Messiah?

If you were there, how much probative value would you have placed in this miracle of feeding five thousand?

Walking on the Water

> *When it was evening, his disciples went down to the sea, embarked in a boat, and went across the sea to Capernaum. It had already grown dark, and Jesus had not yet come to them. (Jn. 6:16-17)*

Well, a few hours have passed. Jesus has not yet shown himself after his sudden disappearance. Since he was gone and the mob could not carry him off to enjoy their adulation, the fickle crowd fell apart one by one to trudge away home. The Twelve and a few more of us closer disciples decided to get back in our boat. We set out for the other side of the sea. Darkness has set in and the sky melted into the waters ahead of us. Funny, but without the comforting presence of Jesus, how dangerous it felt all of a sudden. We are literally a ship without a rudder, because we just guessed we were going to the same place Jesus had gone.

I'm still not sure I want to follow him permanently, and this time without his being with us may help me make up my mind. If he is always going to be with us one moment, and then off on his own somewhere the next, maybe that's not for me. As a member of the council, I know where I am supposed to be and what I am supposed to be doing. Here I have to be incognito lest the other elders find out and turn their ire upon me. It's just that when he is with us, his magnetic personality makes me think of nothing but him. I realize that charm and even unselfish love and care for the helpless has led others in the past to follow men who seemed chosen only to turn out to be scoundrels or charlatans: false prophets. The question for me is: Is Jesus the real thing? Should I commit myself to join Peter and Philip and Andrew and the others, surrendering myself to this band of uneducated fishermen (for the most part)? Should I blindly follow Jesus as they seem to? How often will that mean jumping into a boat as we now just did, setting off for who knows where?

I guess I'm giving him the benefit of the doubt for the moment, or I would not have joined this much smaller group of his followers in setting our for the opposite shore, still not sure we would find Jesus there. The Twelve cannot say for sure we are going in the right direction, but they seem to simply trust that they will find him. Theirs is an infectious kind of trust. Because they have been with him on several such occasions, they seem to take it for granted that they will be led to his next "adventure" if only by the power of his magnetic persona. So now I share this same trust, especially because I am not really at home on the sea, but I am willing to follow their brief commands as to how to find a safe corner of the boat.

Questions

What were Joseph's responsibilities as a member of the Sanhedrin?

In view of that, was he derelict in his duty by spending so much time listening to the teachings of Jesus?

At this point is he still drawn first one way and then the other?

> *The sea was stirred up because a strong wind was blowing. (Jn 6:18)*

Oh, oh. Now my fears are being realized. I'm no fisherman, but I know a storm when I see one developing.

The wind has really picked up. It's getting stronger and producing white caps. There's a pretty strong eddy out there on our left. How much of that can this little boat take? We're pretty far off from shore by now, so that I don't think we can turn back. "Better keep heading into the wind", I hear them shouting. All I know is I'm going to hang on to this rail with all my might and let them get me safely across.

I am not the only one who recognizes trouble on the water. I hear several of Jesus' closest followers among the Twelve, especially the few who were not fishermen by trade, raise their voices in a prayerful tone, calling on Jesus to come save us. Again their trust is evident. It is not that they think we shall really drown or anything that bad, but they call for Jesus to calm their fears as we ride out the storm. After all, we are in this predicament because we are trying to meet up with the Master again. Surely he wants just as much that we succeed in catching up with him, wherever he is…

Questions

Do you think a small inland Sea of Galilee could really raise up such a dangerous storm?

Or is the writer of the Gospel exaggerating a bit to make a point?

> *When they had rowed out three or four miles, they saw Jesus walking on the sea and*

> *coming near the boat, and they began to be afraid. (Jn 6:19)*

Now I'm getting soaked from the waves breaking on the side of the boat. Is this how I was meant to come to an end? They say your whole life flashes before your eyes when the time comes. You lose all sense of time and place. You begin to see things. There, now I see a figure walking on the water and coming toward us. Who is that? Is that my father come out of the grave to take me back there with him? Is that one of the elders with whom I always disagreed in council until he died and is now come to take his revenge? Is it a ghost come to taunt us?

Now all begin to be afraid. Bad enough that the wind and the water are pummeling our poor little boat, but now there is some strange apparition coming toward us. Is this some evil spirit come to punish us for listening to the Teacher? No, it looks familiar. It looks like Jesus! How did he get out here? We are three or four miles on our way and he was nowhere to be seen. How did he get here? He isn't just an apparition; he is moving. He is coming toward us. He does not seem to fear drowning, but we better help him get in the boat with us or one of those eddies will swallow him up. But how can we help him? All hands are rowing hard against the wind, just trying to keep the boat on an even keel.

Questions

Why do the Apostles "begin" to be afraid precisely when they begin to see Jesus walking toward them?

Was an apparition more fearful than a storm?

> *But he said to them: "It is I. Do not be afraid." (Jn 6:20)*

What a sweet voice! How reassuring! Jesus simply identifies himself and thinking of us in our plight, tells us not to be afraid. That could easily be a mantra or motto for Jesus: "Do not be afraid". He has said this to us at other times and to some of those he cured. He always wants to establish a peace-filled environment before he tries to teach us anything or do anything for us. So here he is again. "Do not be afraid." He's the one out in the water and he tells us not to be afraid. He has no business walking on the water, but then if he is the chosen one, he has every right to tread the watery road if it suits him. Foam now covers the feet that Magdalen washed with her tears and wiped with her hair, but he is concerned about us. Several of the others are leaning over the side of boat as if to lift Jesus out of the swirling waves.

Prayers have been answered. We will be safe now that Jesus is with us again. Not that anyone will ever admit that we really were afraid. Timidity quickly gives way to human pride in which we never want to admit our weakness. What kind of foolishness is that? Perhaps this has been another one of Jesus' tests! Has he been testing our trust in him? Has he been testing our fortitude in facing even this kind of adversity in being one of his followers? Was it he who whipped up the storm to teach us ... what? That we need his protection? That we should not have tried to find him, since he wished to be alone? That he is master of the wind and the sea, as he is master of little loaves and fish?

Questions

In what way do you think Jesus was testing the Apostles in this episode?

Or is that too strong a word?

> *They wanted to take him into the boat, but the boat immediately arrived at the shore to which they were heading. (Jn 6:21)*

Now what's happening! A second ago we were struggling to get the Master aboard. But now, all of a sudden, we are not in the middle of the sea anymore.. The boat has somehow reached the shore. The storm has passed; did it hurl us up on the land? No, everything is now calm. Jesus is with us again as if nothing unusual took place.

This is more than my weak heart can endure. When the Teacher told us not to fear, like the others I did at once feel safe and knew he would protect us from harm. And we are now safe ashore. But how did we get here? Did I lose consciousness for the time it took to land the boat?

I now no longer am afraid of the perils of the rough sea, but I am just as upset about these strange and unexplained occurrences. Are you giving us another test, Master? You knew all along how you would be with us on this side of the water, just as you knew all along how you would feed the crowd before you put Philip to the test. You're not making it easy for me to get used to being part of your intimate band of followers. You are really challenging my sense of equilibrium. But there is no doubt that you are Master of material things like bread and wine, and also of the wind and the sea, for these elements quieted when you told us not to fear.

At any rate, we are now together with Jesus again. And the gathering darkness that saw us board our little boat has now deepened to blackness of late night. All is quiet save for the chirping of night creatures in the wilderness that surrounds us. We are bedded under the clear star-filled heavens providing a familiar tent for those who follow the Master, who has nowhere to lay his head.

Despite the exhilaration of the feeding of the multitude and the anxiety caused by the storm I do not find it difficult to close my eyes in the hope of a restful night. I am back in the company of him who said "Come to me and I will give you rest." He is not sure of where my allegiance yet lies; he has not yet spoken directly to me; he has not acknowledged that I am now in his entourage. Yet I feel that peace and rest he speaks of. I am able to sleep deeply and await what the next day shall bring.

Questions

What do you think Joseph thought at this point with regard to his longing to find the Messiah?

If you were there, how much probative value would you find in the way Jesus was able to calm the storm and give peace to his followers?

The Bread of Life Discourse

> *The next day, the crowd that remained across the sea saw that there had been only one boat there, and that Jesus had not gone along with his disciples in the boat, but only his disciples had left. Other boats came from Tiberias near the place where they had eaten the bread when the Lord gave thanks. When the crowd saw that neither Jesus nor his disciples were there, they themselves got into boats and came to Capernaum looking for Jesus. And when they found him across the sea, they said to him "Rabbi, when did you get here" (Jn 6:22-25)*

Oh boy, here we go again. We had a restful night under the stars. Even I had time to calm down from my uneasiness about the trip across the sea. One cannot be with Jesus and remain upset. He exudes confidence and calmness, so that we all were able to sleep the sleep of the innocent, now that he had rejoined us, even if by the strange method he chose to do that. But now we barely had time to greet the new day and partake of some of the left-overs we had collected in those wicker baskets, when now there rises a familiar din coming from the water's edge.

As I look over there, I can see a whole flock of boats has arrived from the other side. I recognize some of the men as having been with us when Jesus fed the crowd. But others seem unfamiliar. I hear them say they live in Tiberias, a town near the place where the multiplication took place. They say they heard about that miracle and have come to see the wonder-worker. I hope they are not just greedy or even just trying to satisfy their curiosity about the Teacher. Though maybe I shouldn't talk – I'm still trying to make up my own mind about him.

They are like me, I guess, because the first thing they do is challenge Jesus about how and when he got here. I don't imagine he will satisfy them with an answer. None of us know how he got here, and we've been with him since last evening. My guess is that he is not fooled by their question, seeming to imply that they are concerned for him and his safety. Even I can see through that. They think they have latched on to a good thing and they do not want to lose it. After all, they wanted to carry him off and make him their king. And no doubt they figure if they were "king makers" then they would benefit from the gratitude of the new king. How can I accuse them of such thoughts? Probably because they were not too different from my own thoughts when I first decided to follow this itinerant preacher just in case he turned out to be the Messiah we had been awaiting!

Questions

Is Joseph fair in his cynical thoughts about the crowd?

Is he perhaps jealous that so many others are implying they have described the Master as the Messiah when he is still not sure himself?

> *Jesus answered them and said "Amen, amen, I say to you, you are looking for me not because you saw signs but because you ate the loaves and were filled." (Jn 6:26)*

No fooling around with the Teacher. He ignores their direct question and instead addresses why they have followed us across the sea. And he makes a great point here; one that confirms my understanding of signs. He says they did not see a sign; yet they did eat the loaves. In other words, they missed the whole point in what he did. He did it to show them he is Master of material things, and therefore more than human. He is doing things in the name of his Father to whom he prayed when he broke the bread. He wants them to see the multiplication as a sign of the approval of his Father, as pointing to his mission from his Father, but they saw only stuff to fill their belly.

I know he is using this as a "teaching moment", because he begins with the phrase "Amen, amen I say to you". That always seems to be his introduction to something that he thinks is particularly important, as a lesson in something to believe. I hope he doesn't berate them too much for this; since I find myself also so slow to catch on. They may be here only to continue to get food without paying for it.

But I wouldn't blame you, Rabbi, if you grow irritated with them and us. Here you were hoping we would see the substance, and we are all enveloped in the mere shadow. Oh, when will we ever learn? How exasperated you could have become. You, the divine artist with a divine masterpiece in your heart, and we foolish critics are praising the simple sketch or outline you make of it! With that same gentle considerateness, that eternal patience, you begin to explain to us.

You don't want others to seek the bread you offered in much the same state of mind. For, how often will they then take advantage of your generosity? How often will they approach your table to partake of your food without thinking about it! All they think of is that this bread cost nothing. And because they will pay nothing, they will get nothing!! Because they will not prepare well enough for this repast, they will come away, not refreshed, but in a stupor, hardly knowing what happened in that precious time! Forgive us, Master, those here in the crowd and then later all those who also may take you for granted!

Jesus, you want us to come in vast numbers to follow you because we have seen these signs and believe in you and accept you and want to follow you on a supernatural basis and all would have been OK. But no – you see we are spiritually blind. We see not signs to an ulterior greatness, but mere wonders of the physical order. And what about those to come after? You are trying to establish the Way, the group of those who believe in your divinity. Will they recognize the signs?

Questions

What do you think of the distinction Joseph posits between the miracle of the loaves and a "sign"?

Is he fair in his assessment of the crowd?

> *Do not work for food that perishes but for the food that endures for eternal life, which this Son of Man will give you. For on him the Father, God, has set his seal." (Jn 6:27)*

You are trying to tell us the purpose of the two miracles which we have just witnessed: the feeding of five thousand and your appearance on the water. They are *signs*, intended by you to prove your divinity, to show us you had the power and the words of life. You claim to be the Son of God and prove your claim by these miracles which are to show us as signs that *"upon him the Father, God, had set his seal."*

These two miracles showed your command over physical laws affecting food and your body and the working of winds and seas. You seem to be making use of our recollection of the distribution of bread yesterday as a jumping off point to speak of a different kind of food. You are using our desire and our need to feed our bodies with the food that you say perishes to teach us about another, more lasting food: one that endures for eternal life. Wow! That will be some kind of food!

When you start talking about eternal life, I think of the other times you referred to a life after death, and that you somehow were going to give us that life. I, for one, am not clear on how you can do this for us. But I now hear you say that the Son of Man – that's you – will give us that special food. . It's not that you are going to tell us where to find it, so that we can get going to get it. We don't have to go anywhere else for it. You will give it to us.

How can we be sure that you can deliver on this promise? Because, you now solemnly aver the Father, God, has set his seal upon you. I don't remember you ever saying so clearly that the Father you keep talking about is God. I may have missed it in the past because I was asleep, or distracted, or not quick enough to read between the lines, especially when you did so much for the unfortunate we have met along the way, "in the name of the Father", as you kept saying. Now you say it distinctly for any to hear who may be listening with an open heart.

This is really as though you are talking directly to me and to me alone. You know I was first attracted to your preaching because you taught an unselfish lesson of going beyond simply obeying the commandments as taught by Moses. You let me be a disciple/follower so that I could see for myself and make up my own mind about your divinity. You know I have followed you in the shadows for fear of the elders. So now you speak openly and state that you are the Son of Man spoken of by Isaiah and the prophets. You declare your Father is God. You say He has set his seal of approval on you. Now I recall being told about the time when the Baptist washed you in the Jordan, and a voice was heard to speak from the heavens "This is my beloved Son, in whom I am well pleased". Yes, Jesus, Son of the Father, I must listen to the rest of what you are telling us about the food for eternal life. I am almost ready to say my search has ended!

Questions

Is Joseph's conversion now complete?

Is he convinced at this point that he has found the Son of God?

> *So they said to him "What can we do to accomplish the works of God?" (Jn 6:28)*

I'm not quite sure I can follow their train of thought here. Except that your use of the word God finally caught their attention. So instead of looking for more bread like what they had yesterday, they now ask about the works of God. Maybe, like me, there are a number in the crowd that are asking you to teach us about God and his expectation of us. After all, that is what a rabbi does, and they did address you as Rabbi. Maybe they are following your lead to move beyond material considerations of hunger and bread and fish to thoughts about God and eternal life.

I certainly hope this is the case, Master. How disappointed you would be if after all the good works and especially the recent miracle in front of this particular group of our brethren, they never did get around to really hearing your words and feeling some compunction to respond to them by seeking further practical advice! It also may be a real turning point in their relationship with you if they are committed to act upon whatever your answer will be. They may be exhibiting real willingness to start getting involved, because their question could open a real bucket of worms, since they are giving you an opportunity to demand sacrifice from them. Could they have moved this much spiritually?

Have I myself made that much progress? To be honest with myself, I do not yet understand what being a follower of Jesus on a permanent basis really means. Does it entail specific duties? Will it mean making drastic adjustments to my daily life? Like them, I also want to know "What must I do to accomplish the works of God?"

Questions

When Joseph asks himself if the crowd has come to accept the sign (and therefore accept Jesus) is he thinking of them or is he projecting his own thoughts on them?

Is he converted yet?

> *Jesus answered and said to them "This is the work of God, that you believe in the one he sent". (Jn 6:29)*

Thank you, Jesus. You are clearly telling them that it is not the work of God to take you off and make you a king, as some of them wanted to do yesterday. God is not sending you to be the kind of ruler they might want to replace our Roman occupiers. He has sent you as one in whom to believe. Faith comes first. You have always pointed that out in the sick you have cured. Their faith has saved them, you keep saying. Now you are telling us faith in you is important for all of us, sick or well or whatever. God's first requirement is that we believe in you.

That should not be hard for me to do. I am already more than half convinced that you have been sent from the Father, for no one has ever done the things you do without being blessed by Jahweh as were the prophets and the kings of our fore-fathers. But that might be an oversimplification of being a follower. There must be more to it than that. If I am to make a commitment, I must know the complete explanation of what you will want from me. I never had the courage to ask outright as some in this crowd are doing, so I'm glad I am here to listen to your further explanation.

Qestions

Does calling belief in Jesus a "work of God" make any sense to you?

Is the word "oversimplification" a logical question for Joseph to ask himself (and Jesus)?

> *So they said to him, "What sign can you do, that we may see and believe in you? What can you do? Our ancestors ate manna in the desert, as it is written, 'He gave them bread from heaven to eat'." (Jn 6:30-31)*

Among us in the crowd, your enemies have mixed with some of the poorer people, encouraging us to murmur "What can you do?" No doubt they had witnessed the loaves and the fishes and their strange multiplication, but in their jealousy that group wants us to think you are an imposter with more than one trick up your sleeve. How easy we are to deceive! But it would take a true miracle to convince those who know better, we are told. Such a true miracle as the rain of manna in the desert. "Do as much, you who gives free bread!" is their attitude, so they call out "Our fathers ate the manna in the desert…"

Inwardly, Teacher, you sigh. Even the manna was a mere figure of what you want to tell us! But you understand our poor minds, and have patience with us. You know we have a keen sense of the relative power and authority of the prophets. You realize that when you said "This is the work of God, that you believe in the one He sent" that you demanded more of us than all the prophets had asked. Complete acceptance of yourself and your teaching.

When you pushed aside the earthly kingdom we wanted for you, your enemies recognized that you claimed power on a supernatural plane, such as no other prophet ever claimed. So, they ask proportionate proof of authority and power. We are to think of Moses – he was the greatest of the prophets, yes. And he proved it by the manna! According to their simple reasoning, then, you would have to be at least good enough to duplicate that one!

You recognize that these challenges are not coming from all in the crowd. You know some of the men who ate with you yesterday were firm believers in your power and even wanted to be subjects of your kingdom, though they saw it as an earthly realm. Still, they are not to be won over by the few in their midst who are your enemies, who are the loudest to shout at you, so you are willing to answer their challenge, using some of their own words and thus not let the entire crowd be turned against you.

Questions

Is it logical for those who have witnessed the multiplication of the loaves and fish to ask for a sign?

Wasn't that in itself a sign? Of what?

> *So Jesus said to them, "Amen, amen, I say to you, it was not Moses who gave the bread from heaven; my Father gives you the true bread from heaven. For the bread of God is that which comes down from heaven and gives life to the world." (Jn 6:32-33)*

The manna gave strength to those who ate of it. It fortified our ancestors and allowed them to continue their weary journey through the desert. So now, Jesus, if I am following you, you want to give us new bread, what you call the true bread, for our daily strength. By this food we are to become good, virtuous, holy. All these virtues are qualities of you which you want us to acquire. So, instead of answering their question directly, you answer our thoughts, our state of mind. You explain to us the difference between physical bread and the bread you bring from the Father, which gives true life, supernatural life. You want to show us that the manna was a figure of the bread you are talking about. *"Instead of this, you nourished your people with food of angels and furnished them with bread from heaven, ready to hand, untoiled for, endowed with all delights and conforming to every taste."* (Wis. 16:20)

Are you telling us we are now to see the realization of this prophecy? That was the first characteristic of the manna: it satisfied the particular needs of each one who ate of it. It had all tastes, was pleasing to all. It supplied for all defects and repaid all worn out energy. That is until, as mere humans, our wandering ancestors became 'tired' of the same food day after day and complained to Moses and Aaron in the face of this great munificence of the Father!

The crowd is slow to follow your point here. While they ascribe the manna to Moses, they know in their heart of hearts that he was only the instrument of Jahweh in feeding our ancestors. You now refer to Jahweh as your Father and you are trying to get us to understand that in this new age, the Father has chosen to work through you to give us the true bread of heaven. What will your true bread do for us? If it is to give us eternal life, it must be a divine antidote delivering us from our daily faults, preserving us from serious sin, and even removing our lesser sins. It must be a burning fire which consumes in the heat of divine love the straw of our spiritual infirmities. It must repair in us the damage done by the sin of Adam and concupiscence. It must restore anything we lose through the attack of the devil and our unruly passions. Your bread must heal the wounds left by the chains of Satan, must point out any weakness where the devil might reenter, and must warn us against the allies of the enemy within our fort (our own evil tendencies).

How is it that I can understand all this in your few chosen sentences? Your words include a deeper message than their surface, literal meaning, as we have seen in previous teachings. If only we stopped letting our predispositions, our biases and selfish concerns get in the way of understanding what you are trying to teach us.

Questions

Did Jesus insult the Jews when he flatly stated that it was not Moses who gave their ancestors the manna?

Is He suggesting that the manna was not true bread?

> *So they said to him, Sir, give us this bread always." (Jn. 6:34)*

Jesus, you have helped the crowd to see we are hemmed in by concepts of bread which can be measured by the loaf. But you are telling us to taste the heavenly texture of this new bread. You want us to always hunger for it. There are two hungers: the desire stemming from need and the desire that is love. We have lived by desires. We seek nothing, undertake nothing, endure nothing, unless we have desired the goal of some endeavor for a long time. Either because we need it and so a loving father works long hours to gain the necessary support of wife and children; or because we love it, and so the hero will brave fire and death to win a beloved.

You recognize in us the desire of need for you in this new bread for it will bring us supernatural nourishment to help us toward a life of perfection. But you want to encourage us to realize we have a second hunger, that which comes from the desire of love, the desire that *is* love, for love is complete only in union. That must be the gnawing sense of emptiness which I have felt; the biting pain of looking for the One I have not recognized, the agony of waiting for what I don't know – all these must be the hunger of love you are telling us about. Just thinking of it makes the tempo of my heart quicken, so that my thoughts all revolve around what you are saying. Unspoken words come tumbling after each other in my mind in a vain attempt to express the emotion I feel that does not proceed in a logical, discursive order, but seeks immediate union with you.

But do the people in this crowd understand that this is what they are asking for when they request to have this bread always? Do they want eternal life or are they still thinking in terms of bodily nourishment so that they will never go hungry again?

I see you as my beloved. I see you as the object of the many hours and days I have felt lonely. I feel a sudden climax to my search for meaning. This bread will allow me to possess you as the object of my desire of love. I want this bread always, Master. I want to be lost in speaking to you about yourself, to be consumed with eternal love of you, for I sense you are telling me that this hunger will never be satiated, and that is the reason you are giving us this new bread – both now and forever.

I join with the crowd in asking for such bread always, whether they are sincere or not.

Questions

Does this sound as though Joseph is completely converted at this point?

Is the crowd asking for the same thing that Joseph is?

> *Jesus said to them, "I am the bread of life; whoever comes to me will never hunger, and whoever believes in me will never thirst." (Jn. 6:35)*

What did you say? The true bread you have been talking about is you?!? So those who come to you, as we have when we follow you, then we have this new bread already? We have you as friend and teacher, so we have this bread? You are speaking metaphorically, then. Not bread to actually consume, but some kind of osmosis whereby we absorb some of your strength and virtues by association with you? What a difference that would make for us. As the manna gave our ancestors the strength to keep moving on through the desert to their promised land, you, our true bread, will be our daily strength. Fortified by you, we can become good, virtuous, holy as we progress through our journey on earth. That is indeed comforting.

Your reply to the crowd is a surprise to them. They ask for this bread assuming it will come in time. But your answer suggests they already have this bread, because we have you with us. They thought they were asking for material food, but you are speaking of some kind of inner nourishment, faith in you. Those who believe in you will receive food that gives perfect refreshment and unending satisfaction. The inner hunger and thirst we have for an unknown something can be appeased, even satiated, through faith.

We thought we were speaking of a day to day hunger for sustenance, but you are speaking of assuaging that fundamental yearning in the hearts of all men for a place of rest. We all seek, by our very nature, a haven of rest. Our hearts are restless until they find that ultimate place of peace, just as our fathers were constantly on the move until they reached the promised land. Faith in you will provide that place of repose. The crowd is not sure whether you are chastising them or what. As for me, I think, Master, that this is what I have been searching for, but I did not know it. Thank you, thank you, thank you!

Questions

Does Joseph comprehend that Jesus is the true bread?

Do you think that the crowd appreciated that Jesus Himself is the true bread He has been talking about?

> *"But I told you that although you have seen(me}, you do not believe". (Jn 6:36)*

So belief in you is the price of having this new bread. And now you are telling us that we do not have that belief. We do not have faith in you even though we have witnessed the things you have done, always in the name of the Father. We question where you came from. We don't know this Father, because we know you are the son of Joseph, the carpenter. I guess you are right. Here am I, a disciple/follower for many months now, a witness to your miracles of curing the sick, of multiplying loaves and fish, a not-too slow-minded leader of my people, and I have still been wavering as to whether I should put all my trust in you. How much less prepared are most of these gathered here to simply take your word for this.

I am sure many of the people thought they believed in you, for they were ready to be your subjects. You are telling us that our idea of belief was to acknowledge the other worldliness of your works. Belief and trust for them and for me until this point has been a kind of surrender to the inevitability of the miracles you perform when it pleases you to work them, and not in them as signs that the Father is working through you. Which really seems strange, for the Scriptures are full of accounts of those favored by God to work wonders in his name, and who were recognized as prophets of the Lord. So why can we not recognize the same in you and believe you when you tell us you have been sent by the Father? Is it because we know where you came from? Is it that you are so much a part of ordinary life in Jerusalem and Galilee that you don't have the aura of one sent by God?

Will you try again to convince us?

Questions

What is it that Jesus wants His followers to believe?

Is this a bit much to ask of people who really were just curiosity seekers?

> *"Everything that the Father gives me will come to me, and I will not reject anyone who comes to me..." (Jn 6:37)*

There's an open invitation if I ever heard one. You are asking us all to have that belief in you. You will accept that faith from any and all who come to you. Even this rabble who were originally thinking only of their stomachs! Even me, a leader of the people, a member of that group of priests and elders who have been doing nothing but trying to kill you! Why? Apparently because it is the Father who is sending us to you. I thought I was the initiator of my following you; but maybe I did not choose you, but the Father started it by sending me to you.

I wonder if certain ones in this crowd who have called you terrible names (blasphemer and the like) can see that you are extending more than an olive branch to them? Can they see that you are most forgiving and willing to forget if they now come to you with an open mind? You insist that you will turn no one away. How understanding you are! How merciful! How loving!

Keep speaking, Teacher. Help us to understand that you must accept all who come to you from the Father, because it is your very mission as the one sent by the Father to lead us back to our Father. You are accepting us as your brothers. You want us to see that what we have in common with you is the desire of the Father that we all are sons of God.

You are really talking about much more than temporary satiety from this true bread. You are claiming it will have the ability to reconcile and unify man and God, as we have never been since the time of Adam. Sinful man has had an instinctive fear of God; from the first man to the present generation, we have "hidden from the fear of God" (cf. Gen. 3:10). How often, Master, have we remained obdurate in our guilt because we are too proud to admit we have been wrong and because we fear to approach God, fear not being pardoned by that awesome Judge?

Questions

How does the Father send souls to Jesus?
What commitment is Jesus here making to the crowd?

> *... because I came down from heaven not to do my own will, but the will of the one who sent me. (Jn 6: 38)*

Was it to disperse those fears that you came down from heaven? Are you the one sent from heaven to bring us back to the Father? In a word, are you the Messiah? If so, you are the one we have been awaiting; but you are also someone of immense power and dignity and heroic virtue –someone I must admit I probably fear more than the Judge.

You have not been using those terms. You still speak of warm, nourishing bread. That suggests continual, repeated, warm and personal friendship, a relationship of intimacy, of love. I find it easier, more comfortable to believe in such a Messiah than in the God of our fathers, who often overwhelmed them with His glory even when leading them through the desert. Calling yourself that bread is so much more appealing; being called our bread makes us feel right at home, for what is more familiar and intimate in our lives than our daily bread?

I guess that is another similarity with the manna you've been reminding us of. It just appeared on the ground with the morning dew. No angel hosts coming out of the sky to deliver it to the amazed people. So you, our warm, kind, forgiving friend are to be our bread – no one to fear or hide from.

Always you speak of your Father's business, doing his will. Now it seems that uppermost in that business is restoring the intimacy between God and man, through belief in you, our daily bread. You have come down from heaven to rehabilitate man, to make us respectable once again. And you are explaining it in terms we can comprehend, by using the metaphor of bread, our daily need.

Hearing your words, it just struck me – you have not come to do your own will, but the will of the Father who sent you. You have repeatedly said you are doing the works of the Father. But that always left the impression of how fortunate you were to have been chosen. The legate of a great king is himself pretty important. The worker of miracles is soon the object of much adulation, as shown by this crowd. But I hear you say that you are not the important one; it is not your will that counts; it is the will of the Father that matters. I hear the refrain from the prophet Isaiah that the Messiah may be a wonder worker, but he is also the Suffering Servant of Jahweh! Not someone calling attention to himself, but a humble, God-fearing savior of mankind.

Questions

What is the second trait of the manna in the desert that occupies the mind of Joseph at this point?

How is coming to believe in Jesus comparable to that second trait?

Was the concept of "the will of the Father" a familiar one to the Jews?

> *"And this is the will of the one who sent me: that I should not lose anything of what he gave me, but that I should raise it (on) the last day".* (Jn 6:39)

If I hear you right now, you are saying that once the Father sends one of us to you, the responsibility is yours to not lose us. That seems a bit unfair to you. Take me: here I have been following you, trying to make up my mind to surrender to your friendship, constantly arguing within myself as to whether I have sufficient proof in the signs you work, vacillating between accepting your message and fearing to burn my bridges behind me; and if I finally turn away, how can that be held against you?

Or maybe I missed something…? Let me review your version of how I get to eternal life, for that is what salvation is:

1. the Father (God) decides to send me to you, asking me to believe in you
2. I respond of my own free will and follow (come to) you
3. You will not reject me
4. You are committed not to lose me
5. I believe in you

6. I will never hunger or thirst again
7. You will raise me up on the last day, i.e., to have eternal life

If I understand this correctly, since you are committed to take care of believers, it would seem the burden is on me to have faith in you. It's really up to me as to how badly I want eternal life. So while you are committed not to lose me, it is still possible for me to freely lose you, so to speak, which would not then be your fault, but mine alone. Jesus, now that I have found you as the object of my desire and the way to life eternal, help me to stay close to you as the source of my salvation.

Questions

Are these seven steps outlined by Joseph consistent with what Jesus has been saying?

Is Joseph completely converted at this point?

> "For this is the will of my Father, that everyone who sees the Son and believes in him, may have eternal life, and I shall raise him (on) the last day." (Jn 6:40)

You have frequently said you have come to do the will of the Father. Now you tell us plainly what that will is. The Father does not wish anything to magnify himself (he obviously does not need that). It is not to create some new earthly empire (though the one we have here now needs to be replaced). His will is not centered on himself – his will is our salvation. The will of the father in sending you to us, Master, is our eternal life. And you are stressing that the way that will is to be carried out is for us to believe in you. What a bargain for us! We have only to believe in you and our reward is to be raised on the last day.

Again you stress the need of faith. Do you do this because you are about to test our faith? Is there more you will be asking of us? Our fathers loved the manna at first, but soon grew tired of it because it was so familiar after awhile. Familiarity did breed contempt with them. Will we become tired of you because we see you too much? Will our new bread become too familiar and our closeness to you become boring? Do we need to believe in something more, perhaps not quite so tangible? Faith, after all is acknowledging the truth of something which we cannot see, feel, touch or demonstrate with our reason or senses. Will you be demanding more than being close to you?

Why do you mention this "last day' again? You know we are all interested in the after life. Our Jewish tradition has trained us all to long for the hope of resting in the bosom of our father Abraham. You now seem to be connecting that hope with our faith in you. And of course our faith in you has been made possible by our mutual love, so we have three virtues connected now: faith, hope and love.

Questions

Does Joseph understand the meaning of faith?

Why does Jesus refer to raising up those who believe in Him on the last day?

> *The Jews murmured about him because he said "I am the bread that came down from heaven" and they said "Is this not Jesus, the son of Joseph? Do we not know his father and mother? Then how can he say 'I have come down from heaven?'" (Jn 6: 41-42)*

I was afraid of this. I had thought myself earlier when you said those words that it was a strange thing to say, since you had been known to work in your father's carpenter shop for many years. What was a friendly explanation of how your very presence with us would be sufficient to sustain us and would lead to eternal life, now has devolved into skepticism due to an idea that contradicts what they know about you, Teacher. I took your meaning to be that you came down from heaven in the sense that your mission was sent by your Father in heaven. Now these fools are hearing only the literal words that you "came down" from heaven when they know you came from Nazareth's carpentry shop. And of course, the enemies in the crowd won't let them hear anything but those literal words. So murmurs arise, a distraction and interruption in what you are explaining. The old story: plant a little doubt in the minds of the weak and they won't see the forest for the trees.

How long will you be patient with us? We are a stiff-necked people, as it was said of our ancestors (cf. Ex. 34:9) – obdurate and hard-headed. Even when being given a promise of eternal life, we cannot seem to rise above our small mind's view of things. At least the murmurs are just from one to another in the crowd; they dare not yell this out to you directly.

<u>Questions</u>

Can you blame the Jews for recalling here that Jesus came from the little town of Nazareth?

Didn't Joseph know that also?

Do you think Joseph is a doubter at this point?

> *Jesus answered and said to them "Stop murmuring among yourselves. No one can come to me unless the Father who sent me draw him, and I will raise him on the last day. It is written in the prophets 'They shall all be taught by God.' Everyone who listens to my Father and learns from him comes to me." (Jn 6:43-45)*

Oh, you did hear their murmuring, after all. Master, you had demanded faith in yourself, and in return promised life, even everlasting life on the last day. I found that comforting. But for this crowd, this was just too much. You had gone too far this time. You lost them when you claimed to have come down from heaven. Those who just did not want to believe seized on this part of your words to cause dissension in the ranks. Why can't they follow your reasoning? Why are they so slow to comprehend? Was it because of their pre-conceived idea of the Messiah as a temporal ruler? Did they find your metaphor as the true bread not earthy enough for them?

You refer to a prophecy about being taught by God. They expect great things when God speaks. How could this former carpenter be chosen as the mouthpiece of God? Preposterous, they are murmuring. When God speaks, it would be through a blinding, alarming, whirling storm, or at least from a fiery bush! It would be when royal kings again sang the psalms, where the people beat their breasts to the verses of the psalter, when another lamenting Jeremiah sat by the waters of Babylon, singing on harp strings which have broken. Without trumpets blaring to announce God's presence, this mob, excited by a few of your enemies, will not listen to you.

Still, you do not hold it against them as a deliberate contradiction to you. Rather, you seem to chalk it up to simple confusion, not outright rejection of your offer. That is so considerate on your part. I would have lost my temper long ago at these constant interruptions to the lesson you are giving!

Questions

Is the answer given by Jesus going to be enough to stop the murmuring?

Would Jesus have been correct to chalk up the murmuring to a state of confusion on the part of His listeners?

> *"Not that anyone has seen the Father except the one who is from God; he has seen the Father. Amen, amen, I say to you, whoever believes has eternal life." (Jn 6: 46-47)*

You are trying to explain that those sent to you by the Father are not up there somewhere in heaven waiting to be sent to you. No one has seen the Father except you. Good point to explain how we are sent to you; troubling point to claim to be the only one to have seen the Father. They won't like that.

But you again solemnly insist that anyone who believes in you will gain eternal life. And that should be the clincher. If they cannot follow the sending and the coming; they ought to get the finale: faith in you assures eternal life. That has to be the central point you are trying to get across, for you have repeated it so often.

Questions

Why would Jesus' claim to be the only one to have seen the Father be troublesome to the crowd?

Is the central point of this discourse so far that faith in Jesus assures eternal life?

> *"I am the bread of life. Your ancestors ate the manna in the desert, but they died; this is the bread that comes down from heaven so that one may eat it and not die." (Jn 6:48-50)*

You have been using a metaphor. Bread gives life; you are bread; therefore you give life; you are the bread of life. That's a good syllogism. But they think you carry it too far when you then start talking about the eaters of manna who died, whereas those who eat your bread will not die. So far we saw the new bread as being an association with you. Now you are talking about eating the new bread. How can we eat the bread, if you are the bread? We are not cannibals!

But that is what you are saying in plain language. You no longer speak of a metaphor, of a figure of speech, of the shadow, of the type – you now speak of something very visible and tangible, even mandible! We are to eat you. You are telling us straight out that you, a concrete person standing before the crowd, a man with human flesh and also the Son of God the Father, will be the nourishment of our souls. Even David and his men who ate the food from the Ark of the Covenant, were still dealing with bread we could understand.

You are the bread of life, you say. Seems a strange

way for you to define yourself. Bread of life. Is it as simple as that? Simple, yes, but not in the sense of easy; rather in the sense of basic. I hear you saying you must be as fundamental, as necessary, as basic to us as bread is to physical life. Bread, then, stands for all we need to sustain life; and you are saying that that is you for us. All we need to gain eternal life. But even for me, who am now totally convinced of what you are saying: how can we eat you? The concept does strain our credulity.

Questions

Why do you think the concept of eating the true bread, which is Jesus Himself, seems to be troubling even for Joseph here?

Is calling Jesus the "bread of life" simple?

> *"I am the living bread that came down from heaven; whoever eats this bread will live forever; and the bread that I will give is my flesh for the life of the world." (Jn 6:51)*

Master, I am trying very hard to follow you. After convincing me that association with you, as though you were some kind of hypothetical bread, would suffice for me to gain eternal life and therefore be reason enough for me to abandon all and commit myself to be a disciple/follower in earnest – now you say this not an analogy; I am to eat your flesh as my life-giving bread. That's quite a jump. Give me time to get used to that idea.

And further you say you are to be the bread of life for the world. That will require some kind of multiplication! Sounds as though you expect the Father to send a very large number to come to you so you cannot lose them, but feed them your flesh to have eternal life. I know you have welcomed any and all to follow you – but the world?! I sense the murmuring has now reached a much more vocal objection to that idea.

Questions

What has happened to Joseph's conversion at this point?

When Jesus says the bread he wants to give them is His very flesh, will that calm any of Joseph's new concerns?

> *The Jews quarreled among themselves, saying "How can this man give us (his) flesh to eat?" (Jn 6:52)*

Oh, how great a challenge you have given yourself, Master. You have carefully built your case with this crowd. After speaking somewhat mysteriously of a new manna of faith that would give life, and of bread that insured eternal life, you finally disclosed the nature of that bread – it was to be your own flesh for the life of the world. At that, I hear bursts of laughter! I hear your enemies taking delight that you showed openly that you are a fool. "Imagine", they shout to the gullible: "feeding the world with his flesh!" The crowd buys their loud complaint: "How can he do this?!" Not that they are looking for an answer to "how"; they use the word to say they think it is impossible, preposterous.

I can see your reaction, Lord. You hear what they are saying. You do not miss the ebbing of hearts away from you. This was your test of them; those small flames of faith that you had enkindled in the hearts of a few are now being blown out by the scoffing of your enemies, unless you find a way to fan them to white hot fire about your promise of life. As you see this inner struggle of common sense against the supernatural sense of faith, you do not mitigate your words in the slightest. Gold must be tried by fire. And if any of us in this crowd are to be among your chosen ones, they must prove their metal by accepting this doctrine. So you go on pouring out to them little short sentences that may seem absurd, unbearable, awful, but true.

Questions

Joseph says the crowd is not really asking Jesus "how" he can do this. Do you accept his interpretation of their questions "how"?

> *Jesus said to them "Amen, amen, I say to you, unless you eat the flesh of the Son of Man and drink his blood, you do not have life within you." (Jn 6:53)*

I know you are trying to help them wrestle with this

unexpected development of your discourse, but I am also trying to assimilate it with what I think I have learned from you heretofore. You told us that it is baptism by water and the spirit that makes us sharers of divine life. And you have preached endlessly that we are to repent and seek forgiveness to restore that life within us if we happen to lose it by disobeying your commandments. Now you say it is by eating your flesh and drinking your blood that we will have life. Does this gainsay what I have learned so far? Maybe not.

You call this the bread of eternal life. Could be that this means a more complete development, a perfection of life that is started in baptism and repentance. That makes sense if I think about another analogy. An infant a day old has life; so too do people who are sick and getting better. But take the suckling away from its mother, and take from the convalescent his special diet, and see how either of them keeps his slender hold on life. So too your flesh and blood are where we get a strong hold on life, for life and the food to sustain it cannot be separated. I guess you are saying "unless you eat this food you will not have life very long!"

Questions

What will be the reaction of the crowd as Jesus now adds to the frightful picture that they must not only eat His flesh, but also drink His blood?

Does the analogy thought of by Joseph help in any way?

> *"Whoever eats my flesh and drinks my blood has eternal life and I will raise him on the last day. For my flesh is true food and my blood is true drink. Whoever eats my flesh and drinks my blood remains in me and I in him!"* (Jn 6:55-56)

Putting aside the first troublesome image of eating your flesh, Master, I see you introducing a further dimension in your presentation. We all know that ingestion of food means we and what we eat are combined; you might even say we are what we eat. So by eating this bread, we are present to you and you to us for more than just the external meeting provides. The encounter with you which I have thinking of all along becomes a more permanent thing this way. We are so united by this heavenly banquet that you cannot lose us as your Father wishes.

You are making the mental images even more strident when you include the idea of drinking your blood in addition to eating your flesh. Of course, they must go together. One cannot partake of the flesh of any animal without at the same time ingesting the blood that is contained in that meat. I guess you are just emphasizing that we are to truly make a meal of your body and associated blood. While I still cannot envision how this will be done, I think I can accept your words and consider it a kind of mystery that perhaps I am not intended to rationally understand.

Questions

Are we expected to accept mysteries that we cannot rationally understand?

Was Jesus trying to confuse them by His strident images?

> *"Just as the living Father sent me and I have life because of the Father, so also the one who feeds on me will have life because of me." (Jn 6:57)*

You have certainly made a point of telling us how close you are to the Father. You are in Him and He is in you. I get the picture that you have life from the father more than any son has been given life through the natural course of siring children. You and the Father share a unique kind of intimacy. And since you call him the living Father, I gather you want us to see that intimacy as much more permanent than normal sonship. You derive life from the Father on an ongoing basis. That is the kind of intimacy you want to have with us also. What a special gift you are offering: one that is comparable to the relationship you have with Him who sent you.

Yes, he has sent you. But you remain in him and do all things because of him and in fulfillment of your mission from him. We are to believe all this by observing the works you do in the name of the Father. All this I have come to accept. Now you have been telling us He has entrusted you with those of us whom he sends to you, and you must not lose any of us. What a unique way you choose to keep that charge. If we eat your flesh and drink your blood we become so much a part of you and you with us that we cannot be separated from you. Is that how all this ties together? There is a certain logic in all this. I don't know yet how you are going to make that happen, but it seems desirable enough that I will wait on further explanation from you.

Questions

Do you see the logic that Joseph says he sees in being called to eat the flesh of Jesus?

What is the state of his conversion at this point?

> *"This is the bread that came down from heaven. Unlike your ancestors who ate and still died, whoever eats this bread will live forever!" These things he said while teaching in the synagogue in Capernaum.* (Jn 6:58-59)

You have said these same final words before. Repetition for emphasis? A final reference to the manna to make us think of your flesh as bread? A mention of our ancestors because you are teaching here in the synagogue? I think I get it, but, beautiful summation that it is, it looks as though not all of the crowd is satisfied. Small wonder! I myself have had a difficult time having the faith you ask of us, and I have been listening to you for some time now.

But many in this crowd are really new to your teaching. They have not been prepared for this radical teaching.

Questions

Why would Joseph refer to this Bread of Life discourse as radical?

Are you surprised that Jesus could have been revealing such a startling offer in the synagogue of Capernaum?

> *Then many of his disciples who were listening said "This saying is hard, who can accept it?"*
> *(Jn 6:60)*

I do not think they mean your words are hard to understand. You have been quite clear. Your words have been concrete, precise and unequivocal. You have stated that your flesh and blood are to be our supernatural food. They just cannot accept because they do not believe in you. Belief, or faith, again is accepting what we cannot see or understand on the word of someone whom we trust. Since many of the crowd do not know how to get above and beyond the merely natural, they do not accept. And they really do not trust you due in part to their short acquaintance with you.

You always know what they murmur about, so you must hear this disavowal also. And I bet it does not surprise you to see their reaction.

Questions

What would the adjective "hard" meant when uttered by these Jews?

Was Jesus not surprised at the reaction of some (or even most)?

> *Since Jesus knew that his disciples were murmuring about this, he said to them "Does this shock you? What if you were to see the Son of Man ascending to where he was before?" (Jn 6:61-62)*

"Shock" is putting it mildly. Some are totally beside themselves. They are disappointed, unnerved and even a little rebellious, thinking you have misled them by now insisting that they accept this weird way to obtain eternal life. "Unless we believe, indeed!" is what I hear all around me. They are so upset at this point that they don't even hear your last question. You want to know if they would believe if you did such a wild thing as rise up into the heavens? The inference being, I guess, that what you are proposing is no wilder than that. This is a second shock wave to their limited thought process. You know many of them have all but rent their garments, but you still try to keep them by going on.

Questions

Was Jesus surprised that His listeners were surprised?

How does Jesus hope to stop their murmuring by asking about His ascension into heaven?

> *"It is the spirit that gives life, while the flesh is of no avail. The words I have spoken to you are spirit and life. But there are some of you who do not believe."* Jesus knew from the beginning the ones who would not believe and the one who would betray him. *"For this reason I have told you that no one can come to me unless it is granted by my Father."* (Jn 6: 64-65)

I sense you coming to a close in this unbelievable lesson. You want to clarify for those who were shocked that your words are spiritual as opposed to the material-mindedness of those who find it a hard saying. They are life giving as opposed to the material which profits nothing. The truth explained in your discourse is the deepest of spiritual truths. If accepted by faith, it becomes the source of life.

You seem to know that it is a lost cause with some of your listeners. You are talking about gaining eternal life, so you remind us that that life comes from the spirit, not the flesh. I take that to mean from the spiritual and not the natural order. You have insisted that it is the Father who sends the chosen to you; so evidently the ones who will not stay to listen any more have not been chosen by the Father and you are letting them off the hook, so to speak. Even in their disgusted shock at what you have proposed, you do not want them to feel it is not entirely their fault that they are so obdurate. They have not been given the gift of faith.

<u>Questions</u>

Is Jesus letting them off the hook by saying that their disbelief is because they were not sent to Him by His Father?

Why does Jesus refer at this point to the one who will betray Him?

> *As a result of this, many (of) his disciples returned to their former way of life and no longer accompanied him. (Jn 6:66)*

It is a shame that it has come to this, Master. I knew the real new-comers were not ready for this wonderful promise based on faith in you. But I see a narrowing of the circle of disciples even among those who have been following you for a time. It seems so many have been following you for earthly reasons: to get material bread free, to be freed from the yoke of our Roman occupiers, to restore the glory of our former Jewish state, and the like. They have decided that you are not the Messiah they hoped you would be. They are so uncomfortable with this teaching that they decide to return to their former way of life, their former occupations, wherein they can find comfort.

As they slink away, you see that your final abandonment has begun. No longer will you have to hide lest the people make you a king. No longer will you have to go out in a boat and preach to the milling crowds that otherwise would suffocate you because of their great number. Ironic, isn't it? They are leaving you because you show how much you love us: by giving your own flesh and blood!

Questions

Would Jesus have resented that many now leave Him in order to return to their former life?

What do you think of Joseph's irony summation?

> *Jesus then said to the Twelve: "Do you also want to leave?" Simon Peter answered him "Master, to whom shall we go? You have the words of eternal life. We have come to believe and are convinced that you are the Holy One of God." (Jn 6:67-69)*

As the men in the crowd left, the shadows lengthened, and the synagogue of Capernaum, trysting place where the love of God was battling the logic of men, grew cold with the fall of dark. In the darkened temple, there remained only twelve disconcerted men who could find nothing to say. But they would not budge. Jesus looks at them one after the other and then comes the question tender, sad, and oh, so human: "Do you also want to leave?"

I am half-way out of the synagogue myself – not to

abandon you, Teacher, but to reflect further on all you have been teaching us. I still wish to see how you are going to give us your flesh and blood. But as I am leaving, I hear your question directed to you closest friends and the reply given by Peter. You are giving them the option of failing the test by leaving with the unbelievers.

"Where else can we find the words of eternal life?" Peter wants to know. Characteristically, Peter is answering for all of them. They have followed you too long to leave you. There can be no other Teacher. Peter has caught on. He recognizes that you speak of life and admits publicly that the way you spoke was the way to everlasting life. His reply indicates he and the others do indeed have the gift of faith which is the prerequisite of staying with you and acknowledging you as the Messiah, the Holy One of God. His words are an example of the unshakeable certitude of faith.

I feel Peter has expressed my own feelings after my many months of trying to find those words. I shall always follow you, Jesus, and maybe now I do not care if the other elders know it. I want to be like Peter! I thank you for the gift of faith.

Questions

Do you think that Jesus expected the Twelve also to leave?

Do you think Joseph's last words signify that he s finally and firmly convinced to accept Jesus as the long sought after Messiah?

PART TWO – THOUGHTS TODAY

A Modern-day Follower's Conversation with Jesus in the Eucharist

✝ Some two thousand years have passed since Joseph of Arimathea might have witnessed the words and actions of Jesus that we have just reviewed. Whether he actually did argue with himself as to the credibility of what Jesus said, and how long it might have taken for him to fully accept Jesus as the Messiah, we do not know. What we do know is that his faith finally was strong enough that he saved the day for Mary and the others on Calvary by seeing to a reverent handling of the dead body of Jesus after His death on the cross. He did have the gift of faith.

Two thousand years later, I have received the same gift of faith. Things are a lot different for me than they were for St Joseph. While I have from time to time met nay-sayers who made fun of my beliefs, I have not had to hide for fear of being physically abused for following Jesus and His church. We do see religious freedom challenged in some of our political pronouncements, but we do not have open religious persecution in our country.

So in this day and age, I am free to enjoy my gift of faith. Further, I am blessed with the opportunity of deepening that faith on a daily basis through reception of the Blessed Sacrament. I need to avoid the pitfall of letting that daily event become trite through repetition. I need to remind myself of the words You used, dear Lord, in announcing to your disciples that You intended to give us Your sacred body and blood as the means to eternal life. As one of your modern day followers, I would do well to recall some of the words You used to convince Your followers in Capernaum that You were, and are, and will be forever, the source of eternal life.

> *"I am the bread of life; whoever who comes to me will never hunger, and whoever believes in me will never thirst." (Jn 6:35)*

I acknowledge that my soul hungers and thirsts for God. I firmly believe that hunger and thirst are appeased by union with You through faith. You recognized that by our very nature we seek a haven of rest. When you promised that those who come to You shall never thirst, You were speaking of such a place of rest. Or, as St Augustine put it, "Our hearts are restless, O Lord, until they rest in You." Only in accepting You and your teachings can we be assured of repose. You seemed to warn us of this condition by suggesting that without the necessary faith, people would not follow You. And as if to prove what You said, many of those who heard Your Eucharistic exhortation did in fact leave You because they lacked faith in You. Without believing in You as the way to everlasting life, how could they possibly believe one of the most difficult of all Your doctrines, one which cannot be proven by anything visible, our sacrament of love!

Questions

Have you firmly and formally told Jesus that you accept His role as Bread of life?

Offer a prayer to Him at this time signifying that acceptance.

"Whoever eats this bread will live forever."
Jn 6:58)

When You said that whoever beholds the son and believes in him shall have everlasting life, You were stressing the need for this faith. It is still important in my day, Lord, that I value this virtue if I am truly to believe in *the* mystery of my faith, the Eucharist. What is merely visible soon grows common and quickly fails to stir emotion. Any face, any scene, however beautiful, loses its stimulating power over us when we become used to it. In the Eucharist there is no human face, no human figure. But there is a presence, which obtains all its power of stimulating my soul, all its emotional control of me, from something much better than ordinary sight; namely my spiritual faith in You.

This is why the Blessed Sacrament never becomes common or usual. There is enough about it that is sensible for our human natural faculties to get a foothold, but the full grasp of it comes from my faith in You. Faith is a supernatural virtue by which we believe a truth above our natural ability to understand on the sole reason that God says it is so. Where else can we find a mystery that is exactly that? In the Eucharist there is only room for pure faith, because we have nothing to go by except the words of God, those memorable sentences that are the essence of the Mass: "This is my body" and "This is my blood". The Eucharist is rightly called "Mysterium Fidei", *the* mystery of faith!

What is the mystery I believe in when I look at You in the host? Actually, there are many mysteries that I accept when I adore You in the Eucharist. There is the miracle of transubstantiation, when I acknowledge that You gave the Apostles and their descendants the power to change bread and wine into Your body and blood: Your real presence in the Host. There is the miracle of the Incarnation, in which I believe this body and blood are You, the second person of the Blessed Trinity, made man by the unconditional Yes of a humble Jewish maiden and the overshadowing of her by Your Holy Spirit. There is the mystery of that Holy Trinity, by which I accept that You are the Son of a loving Father, that the love You two have for each other is Your holy Spirit. There is the mystery of how You can have both a human nature and a divine nature in that one Person. There is the mystery of our redemption, by which I accept that Your death on the Cross, freely offered in accord with the wishes of Your Father, freed us all from sin and death and opened the gates of heaven for us all. There is the mystery of how the sacrifice of the Mass is the same sacrifice as that of the cross, not repeating Your death, but making present in this time and place the efficacy of the death You suffered for all on Calvary. Included in all of these is the mystery of how much You love me.

Questions

Have you ever thought of how all these miracles and mysteries are present in the Sacrament of the altar?

Offer a prayer to all three Persons of the Blessed Trinity acknowledging your faith in all of them.

"I will raise him up on the last day".(Jn 6:54)

When you spoke of raising us up on the last day, you turned our attention from faith to the virtue of hope. During your whole life You hid the power of your divinity so that sinners and children would not fear to approach you. You were goodness and mercy itself. Here in the Eucharist, you are still hidden, but these same virtues shine through so you will be loved and trusted as you were on earth. Here though, it is the interior word that you speak, the language of friendship. It is gentle, considerate, irresistible. As I approach the altar and bow before You, trusting You, I hear You say "Come. I pardon all. Do not fear." Your words are intimate; they penetrate my very heart. And why not, if I come to You, approaching Your omnipotence with simple trust, with the abandon of a child for its parent?

Communion time is this special time of invitation. We would not dare to receive You if we were not invited! I should use the time right before Communion by hearing and answering that invitation, by building up my confidence, my hope. "Lord, I am not worthy that You should enter under my roof" (Communion of the Mass). Examination of self to see my unworthiness is appropriate but almost unnecessary. You know I do not deserve You. Yet You invite me anyway. I hear over and over Your consoling words "Come. I pardon you everything. Do not fear." This preparation alone will make me calm, untroubled, when the big moment comes. Otherwise I'll tremble so much that You will not find rest in my heart.

Questions

Is your proximate preparation to receive Jesus in the Eucharist focused enough on the enormity of the invitation of Jesus to eat His flesh and drink His blood?

Offer a prayer that captures the essence of the prayer at Mass "Lord, I am not worthy…".

> *"Stop murmuring among yourselves". (Jn 6:43)*

When the first Jews who heard you promise your flesh as food for eternal life, they began to murmur about the incongruity of what You were saying. When You come to me in Communion, is your word hindered because of foolish ideas of mine? Do I try to make You fit into my puny ideas instead of listening to what You have come to say to me? You have a perfect right to be annoyed when at Communion time You find I have drawn up my own blue-prints of what we will do together. Where you intended do lay solid foundations of sturdy, substantial virtues like faith, hope and charity, do you find I have laid plans for secondary things? Where You would give much time and attention to the interior spiritual life, do You find me, like the Jews, all taken up with exterior, material ornamentation? Where You would set aside a definite spot for erecting Your austere cross, do You find I have planted there sweet-smelling flowers? When You would transform me into Yourself, do You find me feverishly trying to make You into a figment of my own imagination? If You have to answer "Yes" to any of these questions, I ask for Your forgiveness, dear Lord. Help me to learn that Communion time is *the* time for affective prayer, the time to be calm, relaxed, to taste Your rich life, to listen to You, to Your plans for my life! Remind me that the J-O-Y of Communion means Jesus first, Others second, Yourself last.

Questions

Do you find that the precious few minutes after Communion, when Jesus is actually present in your body, are often lost in distraction or prayers focusing on you instead of on Jesus?

Offer a prayer focusing on Jesus and not on you.

"They shall be taught by God." (Jn 6:45)

When You come to me in Communion, you wish to speak to me. You do not speak to the accompaniment of blaring trumpets. That might be the way at the time of the Apocalypse, but when I receive you into my heart at Mass You speak in whispers, and if I miss any of what You are telling/teaching me, it is lost forever. I cannot afford to miss a single word, a single inspiration, a single lesson.

I sometimes forget this. I make the mistake of constantly talking to You during my Thanksgiving, instead of just loving You. Too much talk on my part paralyzes my communion, which should be the time to deepen our personal relationship. I should listen to you more. It is not the time to search; it is the time to taste.

Communion produces in me a taste for the things of God. I am able to appreciate more the sweetness of Your Heart. I am attracted to the Eucharist and have a facility all of a sudden for seeing everything in relation to the Eucharist. I am one in thought, in attitude, in sentiment with You. As I prayed with the priest at the Offertory of the Mass, "By the mystery of this bread and wine may I come to share in the divinity of Christ…"

I must imitate the bees: they cling to a flower until they find what they need to make their honey; then they fly to the next one. So before turning my attention away from the Lord I have just received, I must extract from every thought the spiritual sugar it contains and form the honey of my affections, my prayers, my resolutions, my work of evangelization.

Questions

What is the essence of affective prayer?

Offer a prayer to Jesus in the Eucharist expressing your conviction that in the Sacrament you share in His own divinity.

"I am the bread of life" (Jn 6:35)

That word "bread" ought to mean something to me. It ought to be the keynote of my attitude in receiving Communion. You come to me as my food. If at times I receive You and do not feel stronger, nourished, it is probably because I am trying to make Communion a heroic act of virtue, forcing myself by many tiresome acts. In a word, I work, instead of eating the bread, rejoicing in Your Sacred Heart. To come to You and tire myself out by too much activity is to miss the whole point of finding rest in You. Not that I should be entirely passive either – I must unite myself to You now within me. But why all the other agitation? One does not go to a banquet to <u>do</u> things, but to eat, to be refreshed. I must stop, then, and taste this heavenly food, this "bread of angels", and remain in contemplation like the angels. Communion is *the* time of affective prayer. If I don't take the time to taste in peace, I will leave the banquet table unnourished. I must stop chattering and allow Your Sacred Blood to course through my veins. You want to be my strength, so I must stop and feel You energize my every faculty, each of my senses, the depth of my heart. How else will You be able to influence my whole day? You come to me, not to entertain me or be entertained by me for 15 or 20 minutes, but to give me strength for the day's battles and duties.

We pray for our daily bread, meaning all we need for life, to be sure, summed up in this very first need, food. So I must look upon You in the Eucharist as my first need, containing all else. My poor human mind is too small to envisage all virtues and graces at one shot. It can only see things one at a time. But, lest I get confused in a maze of parallel lines, You help me to see them all as rays pointing to a single center. You make one grace or gift seem most important, dominant, into which all other graces are dovetailed. This gives my struggle for perfection a special individual character; it simplifies life, connects all my acts, and puts order into the terrible mess of spiritual activity.

This dominant grace lights the whole interior life, shows me my special vocation. It determines my practices of prayer, piety and virtue. It is the motor of all my actions.

It makes my life a patterned continual whole. One soul has the grace of devotion to the Passion – Your sufferings are its constant thought; its virtues, its love, its life is dominated and inspired by the Passion. Another soul has a special attraction for penance; every action for that soul will have a penitential character. Perhaps the most excellent of these special graces of attraction is seeing all summarized in You as bread of life. I feel that is the case with my devotion to you.

Many souls have been given a special attraction to the Blessed Sacrament, especially those who live a life of religious perfection. This is not surprising for this devotion is a little easier, and more at hand, as it were, since the means for developing it are close to them as they practice their vows. They even live under the same roof as You constantly.

I feel a similar facility for having this special devotion, even though I live "in the world". Maybe because devotion to You in the Blessed Sacrament is more attractive from a human standpoint. As for other special devotion or graces: take the Passion, for instance. Great faith and love are needed to keep close to such a mystery, past and distant as it is. And separated from Communion, the Passion is only immolating and crucifying; whereas devotion to the Eucharist is a grace of sweetness, of deepening love. I find it easier for me to lose myself in love than in suffering. Not that the Eucharist is not tied up with the Passion – it is, of course! But it is also tied up with Bethlehem, with Nazareth, with Galilee, for through the Eucharist all the mysteries of Your life are made real and present and actual for me today.

It is the glorification of all Your mysteries, all Your virtues and perfections. When you say "I am the bread of life", You sum up in the Eucharist all the marvels of Your divine person, of Your two natures. Not only that, but in itself, the object of this devotion is the most noble, for it is the very Body and Blood and Person of You Yourself. You are here closer to me that at any other time. The flame of Your love consumes the flame of my love and each burns by the fire of the other. That is real union!

Questions

At Communion time, do you feel a special closeness to Jesus, the Word made flesh who devised a way to be with us physically even after His glorious ascension into heaven?

Offer a prayer expressing your gratitude for the wonder of this sacrament of unity.

> *"I am the living bread that came down from heaven". (Jn 6:41)*

You are stressing here that you are living. That is, You not only give me life, but You live in the Eucharist Yourself. You are in the Eucharist not only to distribute Your graces, but above all, to be my path and model. Only in the Eucharist are the virtues easily learned and copied. I can observe them the way You practice the virtues You showed us centuries ago. You are there – the gospel come alive. When I read the gospel, which is a dead history, I visualize the same virtues being lived now at this very moment in the Eucharist. My power of understanding is much greater and the meaning of the Gospel is much clearer.

Thanks to the gift of the Eucharist I have before my eyes the continuation of what I am reading. Of course, you are practicing these virtues in a hidden and invisible way now. So I, as all spiritual writers show us, must take the pains to see and figure out just how You are humble in the Host (hiding Your divinity); obedient in the Host (coming at the call of the priest); patient in the tabernacle (waiting for our visits), etc. But what will be most profitable will be to see You practicing the most important virtues: adoration and love of the Father, reparation for sin, thanksgiving and continual recollected prayer. That is how You spend Your time. "Not a very active life" one might think? To the contrary, that is *real* living. That's the kind of life You have Yourself and want to impart to me. If I join You in these virtues when You are in my heart, maybe that will be a head start to doing it all day long.

And when You do come down to me at Communion time, how do I act? How do I spend my thanksgiving time? I realize thanksgiving should be more than reciting a set of "acts" of various virtues, for that is the way we taught children to give thanks. Their little minds are so easily distracted; they have to be trained in spiritual exercises; their developing minds do not yet know how to be totally recollected. But I'm supposed to have grown out of set "methods". Lord, let me just remember the simple fact that I have in my heart a friend. Simple courtesy will then demand that I listen to You. You will not be looking for me to make excuses for my faults, for "acts" of sorrow, of amendment and so forth. Friends do not visit in order to reproach. They do not begin with speeches. So neither do you, Lord; so our first minutes together should not be pre-occupied with that.

A rich man or a king visiting a peasant would not begin with a loud proclamation of his power and riches compared to the poor man's misery. He has probably come to alleviate that distress, to help the poor wretch forget his troubles. So it is with You, Lord Jesus. You come in Communion as a familiar. You give here the greatest sign of Your love, sweetness, goodness, gentleness, intimacy. The familiarity of a tete-a-tete. Your soft voice has said "Come to Me". So when I have you in my heart, I should keep the same confidence, hear that same word of welcome, and think of nothing else. I don't need the method any more. I will be surprised at how readily You take over the conversation. You know what is on my mind already, so all I have to do is listen!

Questions

Have you ever thought of Jesus practicing virtues in the Eucharist?

Offer a prayer committing yourself to grow in one or more of these virtues in imitation of our Eucharistic Lord.

> *"... and the bread that I will give is my flesh for the life of the world."* (Jn 6:51)

What kind of a life am I trying to live? One that is modeled on Your own. But You are God – how can I live like You? I remember reading somewhere that such a doubt is reasonable for us frail humans. But You have taught us that I can attempt to emulate You by the power of the Spirit when He is pleased to dwell within me. It is by virtue of this divine Spirit that I may attempt to live a life like Yours, living the virtues and doing the works of God and not of men.

Does that mean I want to live a life full of wonders? No; rather a life that is simple, that is focused on the will of the Father, that is absent of self. I think that is what is meant by a "hidden" life –one where the big I is kept in its place. Despite your miracles and wonderful preaching, you really led a hidden life. Even now you hide your divinity and Your humanity under the insignificant species of bread and wine. Your wisdom doesn't pronounce divine sentences. Nothing appears of Your power and glory in this small Host. To be poor, small, simple – that is the life of the Eucharist, so that is the kind of life I want to live.

Poverty, meekness, patience – that is the kind of life You show me and You invite me to live. How considerate on your part. You know that occasions for heroism are few and far between, that most of us are called to live simple lives. In small things we must find our sanctity. Your emptying Yourself of Your divine prerogatives shows me that the interior life, composed of acts of the heart and beats of love and union of intention is the most perfect way for me. Following Your example, I am called to be a man of interior life, finding my special sanctity in practicing interior recollection and concentration on an intimate union with You and the Father through the Spirit. The truly interior man can work for souls while remaining recollected. Hidden! Interior! United!

Questions

How can focusing on the development of a more perfect union with Jesus in the Eucharist prepare one for the work of evangelization to which we must all be committed?

Offer a prayer to Jesus committing yourself to an interior life of love.

> *"Unless you eat the flesh of the Son of Man and drink his blood, you do not have life within you". (Jn 6:53)*

Life and the food to sustain life cannot be separated. I'm still trying to focus on what kind of life this should be. Life is not something to be acquired and put in a gilded cage like an antique. It is to be used. And the constant use results in wear and tear, which therefore calls for a continual repair job to be done. The holier life I try to lead, the greater my need for frequent Communion. A holy life, a pure life, demands more sacrifices, greater struggles. Therefore I need more strength. When we have a lot of work to do, a long journey to take, we have to eat a good amount ahead of time. Communion is the only way to fortify myself for the work of daily supernatural living. If it were given to us as a reward for our virtues, if we had to be holy men and women before we were worthy or able to receive You, then we could live without You; we would be holy already. But precisely because we cannot live without You, we see that we need You, and are not worthy of You.

The manna in the desert was also a bread of peace, sweet to the taste and causing joy among our ancestors. What then must be the true bread you are giving us? Joy and happiness are simply the possession of good; but you tell us that in your bread we are to receive the infinite Good. The soul recollected in its thanksgiving feels a certain elation caused by the presence of this Good, a force of union with God. We are to feel You in our whole being and consider ourselves a paradise inhabited by God, where we will join the praises, thanksgiving and benedictions sung by the choirs of angels and saints. You will make us feel free from the exile in this valley of tears, as we repose in your loving heart.

For you know that we need from time to time to taste the sweet side of your love. We cannot forever be doing battle with Satan. So you come to us as in a time of respite, a precious time when all else is suspended. Time will stand still. You will be enjoyed and loved and possessed as you will be in eternity forever. It is this joy which leads to real love. We love only what makes us happy. We will not find that complete happiness anywhere else. We must then eat this bread you offer to us. "Taste and see how the Lord is sweet" said one of our prophets. The sweetness of unending joy. That is what you mean when you tell us this is the Bread from Heaven, which gives everlasting life.

How easy it should be to love humility when we see the God of glory humble Himself to come to our miserable hearts! How easy it should be to admire docility and meekness when we have within us the meekest of all hearts! How lovable the neighbor should be when we find him next to us at the divine table, loved with the same great love of Jesus!

Questions

How often have you thought about the Eucharist as food?

Offer a prayer to Jesus, telling Him what you understand about His flesh and blood being the source of your life.

> *"Whoever eats this bread will live forever."*
> *(Jn 6:51)*

And the life we shall live will be the one that is natural to You who are our food – a life of prayerful love. Jesus, You are love, and all our life, since we receive You so often, must be one of developing Your love. You do not show Yourself in body and blood in any visible way precisely so that we will have to look for something else, something deeper and more important: the love of our heart. And when we find Your heart, we will find it busy praying. You would not give Yourself entirely to an active exterior life. All through Your human life You kept going apart from the world, hiding yourself to pray and contemplate. Have we a richer treasure of graces than You somewhere, a source of solid strength that gives us the privilege of not following Your example? Hardly! No matter what our service to You and Your people might be, all will be vain and sterile unless we learn to feed on Your heart, your strength, through prayer.

In the Eucharist is where I can find the example of all those virtues I am trying to practice. I wish to be penetrated by Your example. Where else will I find a greater love of humility if not at the feet of Your sacred heart? Where can I find a better example of silence, recollection, patience, sweetness? Any piety which does not feed on Your life, Your prayerful love, will be sterile. I think that is the kind of life you want me to live, which you desire to bring to me through eating of Your flesh and blood. When I receive You, Lord, I ask for Your body and blood to course through my veins to assimilate my life blood and enrich it and make it live Your life of prayer, of love, of virtue. No other kind of life would be worth living forever, which is the only kind You promise to make eternal through reception of this Blessed Sacrament.

A life of love is what You want me to have. You gave us only one commandment: to love one another. While I try daily to keep that commandment, I must admit that it is difficult at times. Loving my spouse, my children, my extended family, my close friends – that isn't too hard. It's the quarreling co-worker, the meddlesome neighbor, the overly ambitious acquaintance, not to mention the know-it-all political pundit and even the constantly complaining fellow parishioner that are difficult to love as You want. It's the pan-handler that accosts me in the parking lot, the homeless person who is careless about my property rights, the welfare person flaunting food stamps at the grocery store. Where will I get the courage to keep trying to show love toward such as these? I hear You telling me I can only live such a life by eating Your flesh. Meditating on how unworthy I am to be united with You in this way will help me not to judge these "hard to love" people, because You love them as much as You love me.

"We have come to know and believe in the love God has for us. God is love, and whoever remains in love remains in God and God in him" (1John 4:16) That sounds as though my life without loving all of those people, and others I have not even encountered yet, is not the life you want of me. For my special union with You to remain, I must love everyone.

Questions

Have you found difficulty in loving some of the people enumerated above?

Offer a prayer to Jesus in the Eucharist asking for

guidance in showing love for everyone with whom you come into contact in your daily life.

> *"Whoever eats my flesh and drinks my blood remains in me and I in him". (Jn 6:56)*

Besides Your physical dwelling in me during the few minutes after Communion, there is the habitual state of intimacy with You possessed by those who receive You often. It is a question of being "recollected" with You, of turning from the outside to the inside. Recollection, we are told by ascetics, as understood in respect to the spiritual life, means attention to the presence of God in the soul. It includes the withdrawal of the mind from external and earthly affairs in order to attend to God and Divine things. It is the same as interior solitude in which the soul is alone with God.

This has very practical consequences. If I am recollected in this way, when I am asked to do something, my first thought is not to see if it is convenient personally, if it is advantageous to me. Rather my first thought is to consult You, Lord Jesus, to know if the thing pleases You, if it will procure Your glory. My frequent aspiration is "Lord, may my every thought, word and deed tend to Your greater glory". If so, that will make me happy. Happy, if in order to please You, I have to renounce myself, make some little sacrifice. Happy when love of You becomes an habitual thought, when it becomes the control of all my passions and desires, when my heart is sad without You.

How do I get to this stage of recollection? By practice. By centering my attention all day long on how You would react in such and such a circumstance. By being Christ-centered and not self-centered. By trying to live in the will of the Father as You always did.

<u>Questions</u>

Can the concept of a life of recollection help you to remain united to Jesus long after the few minutes of unity immediately after reception of Communion?

Offer a prayer to Jesus in the Eucharist asking for a deeper life of recollection to keep all your thoughts, words and actions united to the will of the Father.

> *"The words that I have spoken to you are spirit and life". (Jn 6:63)*

A life of love is what You promise to give me if I receive the Eucharist properly. Every human heart pursues some sort of love. But the love to which You are calling me is the noblest of loves, because in sharing Your divinity in Communion, I must love as You did. How was that? The gospels stories I hear at Mass every day are full of how much You loved us. That heart which gave its last breath on Calvary to make it possible for me to enter heaven has not changed in the Eucharist on the altar. It still beats for me. You love me personally. You want to deepen our personal relationship. It is that love for each of us that I want to imitate. You want me to bring Your love to others.

Your gift of spirit and life are not meant to lay fallow in my soul – I am to share them with those around me.

Questions

Does the concept of a personal relationship with Jesus help you to be more focused on Him at Communion time?

Offer a prayer to Jesus expressing your intention of deepening that personal relationship with Jesus.

> *"No one can come to me unless the Father who sent me draw him." (Jn 6:44).*

You have stated clearly that faith in You and Your Eucharist are a gift of the Father. How fortunate I am to have been thus favored. In moments of refection and meditation I have at times dreamt of sharing somehow the great privilege that was Mary's when within her womb lay the incarnate Son of God during those months of intimate union. Again I dreamt of the wonderful grace whereby the beloved disciple John was allowed to lovingly lay his head upon the breast of his Master in such a joyful, close familiarity with the most beautiful of the sons of men. Too, I have dreamt of those fortunate children whom You took on Your knee while You spoke to them kindly and gently laid your arms around them and looked down with love at them so they could see their own smiling faces reflected in Your bight eyes.

If I had the happiness of taking part in any one of

these scenes, I would be transfixed forever, the memory of that glorious experience always vivid in my mind. But what are such external things when compared with the inner union which actually is mine! How fortunate I am to have been given the gift of faith in You by our heavenly Father. Why He chose me, I do not know. There are countless souls in this world who have not been given such a calling. Surely it is not because I am more worthy than they. Perhaps You will call them in another way? All of this only makes the mystery of the Eucharist more mysterious. I shall never comprehend this mystery. You have told us that the ways of God are not the same as the ways of man; that as high as the heavens are above the earth, so much of a distance is there between Your ways and mine.

In sum, You wish to abide in me and I in You. Through eating Your flesh and drinking Your blood, I forge a special union with You - a union more splendid, an intimacy more lasting, a friendship surpassing any of my dreams. And it is mine in Holy Communion!

Questions

How often have you thanked God for the gift of faith?

Offer a prayer to the Father in heaven for the gift of faith that has singled you out from so many others and permits you to come to Jesus.

Epilogue

We have attempted to visualize the events of Chapter Six of St. John's gospel by imagining how they may have brought about a belief in the divinity of Jesus on the part of one of His secret followers, Joseph of Arimathea. We also have listened to a modern-day follower converse with Jesus in the Eucharist at the time of receiving Him in Holy Communion. And we have sought a deeper understanding of this most difficult chapter by answering challenging questions throughout our meditation on these events.

A final distinction may be helpful in carrying away an important element of studying this or any of the gospels. That is the distinction between being a follower of Christ and being one of His disciples.

Joseph of Arimathea accepted many of the teachings of Jesus and was therefore a follower of the Lord. When he finally understood the real nature of the relationship that Jesus was inviting him to share and accepted Jesus as the Bread of Life, he became a disciple.

When we accept the teachings of Jesus, the doctrine involved in being a Christian, we are followers of Christ. But to be a disciple is to know Jesus as a person, to enter more deeply into His life and thus enjoy a loving, personal relationship with Him.

TO JESUS THROUGH MARY!

TRUE DIRECTIONS
An affiliate of Tarcher Books

OUR MISSION

Tarcher's mission has always been to publish books that contain great ideas. Why? Because:

GREAT LIVES BEGIN WITH GREAT IDEAS

At Tarcher, we recognize that many talented authors, speakers, educators, and thought-leaders share this mission and deserve to be published – many more than Tarcher can reasonably publish ourselves. True Directions is ideal for authors and books that increase awareness, raise consciousness, and inspire others to live their ideals and passions.

Like Tarcher, True Directions books are designed to do three things: inspire, inform, and motivate.

Thus, True Directions is an ideal way for these important voices to bring their messages of hope, healing, and help to the world.

Every book published by True Directions– whether it is non-fiction, memoir, novel, poetry or children's book – continues Tarcher's mission to publish works that bring positive change in the world. We invite you to join our mission.

For more information, see the True Directions website:
www.iUniverse.com/TrueDirections/SignUp

Be a part of Tarcher's community to bring positive change in this world! See exclusive author videos, discover new and exciting books, learn about upcoming events, connect with author blogs and websites, and more!
www.tarcherbooks.com

CPSIA information can be obtained at www.ICGtesting.com
Printed in the USA
LVOW08s0700240215

428015LV00001B/1/P